GREETINGS FROM SOMEWHERE

The Mystery of the Stolen Painting

BY HARPER PARIS • ILLUSTRATED BY MARCOS CALO

LITTLE SIMON

New York London Toronto Sydney New Delhi

entire story or passage is completed. If students are not following your prosodic flow, repeat the echo reading a second time. Provide students with feedback.

Progress Tracking
- Record the students' progress each time this technique is used. For example:

Tracking Progress for Student: _____			
Technique # 3 – Echo Read – Characteristics of Prosody			
Text	**Date:** _____	**Date:** _____	**Date:** _____
1. **Intonation**	✓		
2. **Stress**			
3. **Punctuation**	✓		
4. **Flow**	✓		
5. **Phrasing**			

Curriculum Based Measurement: Oral Reading Fluency Probe, pages 198-200.

Sources:
Rasinski, T. V., Padak, N., Linek, W., & Sturtevant, B. (1994). Effects of fluency development on urban second-grade readers. *Journal of Educational Research, 87,* 158-165.

Carnine, D. W., Silbert, J., & Kame'enui, E. J. (1997). Direct instruction reading (3rd ed.). Upper Saddle River, NJ: Prentice-Hall.

Fluency — 4:
Paired Read Aloud

What it is: A technique to develop fluency through repeated reading.

When to use it: When students need to develop reading rate, phrasing and expression.

⚠ A prerequisite is the ability to read at the primer level or higher.

Benefit: Students learn collaboration skills as they give and receive feedback with peers regarding reading fluency.

Materials:
- An unfamiliar passage for each student at his or her reading level; passages should be between 100-200 words
- Timer
- Copies of Fluency Feedback Form, page 237.
- Oral Reading Fluency Probe, pages 198-200.

Implementation Steps:
1. Rank students by reading ability from high to low based on your classroom assessments. Divide the list in half. Pair the highest-level reader from the first half of the list with the highest-level reader from the second half and continue until all students have a partner. Keep the partners the same each time this activity is used until the next assessment (at which point ranking will probably have changed).

2. Prior to implementing this activity the first time, have students generate a list of unique words and phrases they can use to acknowledge/compliment each other. Post the list in the classroom where it is visible for reference. Some example compliments might include:

    "Wow, you read that like a star!"
    "That was an awesome reading of the book!"
    "You slam-dunked that passage!"
    "Your expression made the story interesting!"

Stress to the students that complimenting means no criticism or advice is allowed.

3. Explain that this activity will involve listening to a partner read a passage for one minute, three times and providing fluency feedback after the third reading. The feedback will include completing a form and reviewing it with their partner.

4. Model fluent and non-fluent reading for the class. Demonstrate the differences between smooth and choppy reading and what reading sounds like with and without expression.

5. Provide students with the Fluency Feedback Form, and a copy of the passage you are going to read aloud. Set the timer for one minute, read the passage and have students follow along. Instruct the students to mark the last word you read when the minute is up. Repeat this process three times. After the third reading have the students complete the form and review their feedback with you. Be sure to have them give you some compliments! This familiarizes them with both the Form and the activity.

Partner Name: _____

After the 3rd reading, my partner…..   **Compliments**

☐ **Read more words**

☐ **Read smoother**

☐ **Read with expression**

---

6. Now have the partners sit next to each other and establish who will be the reader first and who will be the listener. Provide each student with a copy of his or her own passage and a copy of his or her partner's passage along with a Fluency Feedback Form. Explain to the students that if they finish before the timer goes off they

are to go back to the beginning and read the passage again. The listener should make note of this on the feedback form. Set the timer for the first one-minute reading. The readers read their passages aloud to their partners. The listeners follow along and attend to the partner's expression and smoothness. At the end of the timing they mark the last word read. Repeat this exercise twice. After the third reading the listener completes the Feedback Form and then shares the information with the reader.

7. The partners change roles and the process is repeated.

8. If desired completed forms can be collected by the teacher for review.

Note: Watch for students who may require longer reading passages and plan accordingly.

Variation: Have students engage in a two to three minute retell about their passage after the third reading. This develops students' understanding that reading with fluency is about comprehension.

Curriculum Based Measurement: Oral Reading Fluency Probe, pages 198-200.

Sources:
Herman, P. (1985). The effect of repeated readings on reading rate, speech pauses, and word recognition accuracy. *Reading Research Quarterly, 20,* 553-564.

Pressley, M., & Afflerbach, P. (1995). *Verbal protocols of reading: The nature of constructively responsive reading.* Hillsdale NJ: Erlbaum.

Koskinen, P. S., & Blum, I. H. (1986). Paired repeated reading: A classroom strategy for developing fluent reading. *The Reading Teacher, 40,* 70-75.

National Dissemination Center for Children with Disabilities (NICHCY). (2007). *Fluency and comprehension gains as a result of repeated reading.*

Fluency — 5:
Fluency Checks

What it is: A technique to increase reading rate.

When to use it: When students require practice reading connected text fluently.

Benefit: Students chart and track their own fluency progress.

⚠️ A prerequisite is the ability to read connected text independently, at least 20 words per minute.

Materials:
- Reading passage containing 150 or more words at the students' independent reading level
- Manila folders
- Copies of Data Collection Sheets, page 239, and/or Graphing Charts, pages 212-215, for each folder
- Blank transparencies
- Transparency pens
- Masking tape
- Timer
- A transparency of each of the following: a reading passage, the Data Collection Sheet, page 239, and a Graphing Chart, pages 212-215.
- Oral Reading Fluency Probe, pages 198-200.

Implementation Steps:
1. Provide the student with a reading passage at his or her independent level, along with a Data Collection Sheet, a Graphing Chart, and a manila folder that has been put together in the following way:
    - Place Graphing Chart on the front outside of the folder
    - Line up the top of the chart with the fold so it fits on the cover; staple the four corners
    - Open the folder, place the transparency on the right side and fasten it to the folder by taping it on the left along the fold

2. Allow students to personalize the folders with their name and artwork. Explain that the folders are for storing data sheets and reading passages. The charts will be used to plot their data and keep track of progress. The reading passage slides under the transparency to permit reuse. Let the students know that the data and the charts are for personal review and will not be used to assign grades or for comparison with peers.

3. Explain to the students that they will be given two, one-minute opportunities to read aloud for practice and then will read aloud a third time for the "one-minute fluency check." After the third reading they will chart their reading rate.

4. Demonstrate the process by placing the passage transparency on an overhead. Set an audible timer for the first one-minute read aloud and read the passage. Repeat this a second time. Now repeat a third time and at the end of this minute, circle the last word you read and show the students how to count the total number of words read in the minute. Finally, show the students how to record the score on the Data Collection Sheet and then how to place that same information on a chart. For example:

Progress Tracking:
- Use the Data Collection Sheet and Graphing Chart to keep track of student progress.

Data Collection Sheet

Name:				
Date:	1/1/07	1/10/07	2/01/07	2/09/07
Passage	Level D # 1	Level D #1	Level D #1	Level D #2
Score wpm	41 wpm	43wpm	45wpm	44wpm
Goal:				
Date:	2/25/07			
Passage				
Score wpm				
Goal:				

Graphing Chart

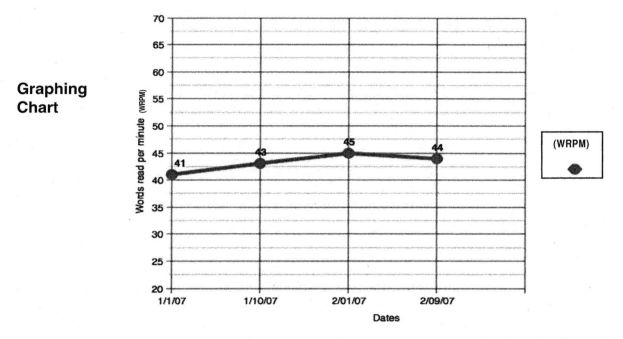

5. Next the students will read. Tell them to get ready for the first practice read. Let them know you will say, "please begin" when you start the timer and will instruct them to stop reading at the end of the timing. Provide feedback if necessary during this time.

6. Repeat Step 5.

7. Inform students that the next reading is the fluency check, and that the results of this reading will be recorded. Encourage students to do their best reading, not their fastest. Tell them to use their transparency pen to circle the last word read when time is called. Repeat Step 5 without feedback. After you say, "stop reading," have them count the number of words read, record the date and that number on the Data Collection Sheet, and then transfer that information to the Graphing Chart to visually illustrate their scores.

8. You can verify the students' data by listening to them during the fluency check.

9. Clean the transparencies with water in preparation for the next fluency check. When the students become familiar with a given

passage or when they achieve a higher independent reading level, replace with a new passage.

10. After at least three data points have been collected, help the students set either a long-term (10-12 week) goal of words per minute read or an improvement goal of reading more words each week. For example:

Student – Joe				
Date:	12/15	12/22	1/5	
Score wpm	57	59	60	
			Goal +1.5 wpm/wk	

Student-Joe   Grade: 2   Date: Jan 5th
Current reading rate: 60 wpm
My long-range goal is: 80 wpm by April 15
OR
My short-term goal is: 1.5 wpm more each week

Note: Personal goal setting can be an intrinsic motivator for students. It allows them an opportunity to challenge themselves during the fluency checks. The charts below (Fuchs & Fuchs, 1993) show expected reading rates by grade level and word per week growth rates for goal setting.

Reading Rates By Grade Level	
Grade	Words per minute
1st grade spring	50-70
2nd grade fall	70-90
2nd grade	90-100
3rd grade	100-120
4th grade	120-140
5th grade and up	140 +

Realistic Growth Rates	
Grade	Words per week
1	2
2	1.5
3	1
4	.9
5	.5

Variation: Students can be paired up for fluency checks. To do this, assign students in the following way: rank the students by reading ability from high to low based on classroom assessment. Divide the list in half. Pair up the highest-level reader from the first half with the highest-level reader from the second half and continue until all students have a partner. Keep the partners the same until the next assessment changes the ranking of the students.

Curriculum Based Measurement: Oral Reading Fluency Probe, pages 198-200.

Sources:

Samuels, S. J., Schermer, N., & Reinking, D. (1992). Reading fluency: Techniques for making decoding automatic. In S. J. Samuels & A. E. Farstrup (Eds.), *What research has to say about reading instruction* (pp. 124-144). Newark, DE: International Reading Association.

Freeze, D.R. (2001). *Precision reading: Instructors' handbook*. Winnipeg, MB: D.R. Freeze Educational Publications.

Suggested Resources for Fluency

Adams, G. & Brown, S. (2003). *The Six Minute Solution: A Reading Fluency Program.* Longmont, CO: Sopris West Educational Services.

Beck, R. Conrad, D. & Anderson, P. (2005).*Practicing Basic Skill in Language Arts: One-Minute Fluency Builders Series.* Longmont, CO: Sopris West Educational Services.

Birsh, J.R. (1999). *Multisensory Teaching of Basic Language Skills 2nd Edition.* Baltimore, MD: Paul H. Brooks.

Carnine, D. W., et al. (2005) T*eaching Struggling and At-Risk Readers, A Direct Instruction Approach.* Newark, NJ: Pearson.

Mathes, P. G., et al. *Peer Assisted Literacy Strategies (PALS).* Longmont, CO: Sopris West Educational Services.

Rasinski, T.V. (2003). *The Fluent Reader, Oral Reading Strategies for Building Word Recognition, Fluency, and Comprehension.* New York, NY: Scholastic.

Vaughn, S. & Linan-Thompson, S. (2004). *Researched Based Methods of Reading Instruction, Grades K-3.* Alexandria, VA: Association for Supervision and Curriculum Development.

Chapter 8
About Vocabulary

"Words are your wheels to take you anywhere you feel."
—Brooks and Dunn, *Words Are Wheels*

Vocabulary, the knowledge of words and word meanings, refers to the words we know that enable us to think and communicate our needs and thoughts. "Vocabulary knowledge is knowledge; the knowledge of a word not only implies definition, but also implies how a word fits into the world" (Stahl, 2005, as cited in Heibert & Kamil). Vocabulary knowledge is cultivated over the course of a lifetime. It is acquired through incidental exposure to words in one's environment and through intentional, direct instruction. Each of us creates our own lexicon, our personal reservoir of vocabulary, of knowledge which begets our ability to communicate.

> **"Vocabulary … the knowledge of a word not only implies definition, but also implies how a word fits into the world" (Stahl, 2005).**

There are several ways to conceptualize vocabulary. Terms such as receptive vocabulary and expressive vocabulary are prevalent in the world of communication. Cummins (1979) defines vocabulary knowledge as words necessary for basic interpersonal communication skills (BICS) and words for cognitive academic language proficiency (CALP). We eventually delineate two types of vocabulary: oral vocabulary, the words we use when speaking or listening; and print vocabulary, the words we recognize or use in reading and writing (Lehr, Osborn & Hiebert, 2003).

We have chosen to cite a few of the numerous research studies that have verified our own belief: in order for students to comprehend what they are reading, they must understand what the words mean. The National

Reading Panel (2000) upholds that children who begin school with a wealth of vocabulary knowledge (i.e., many words from print in their oral vocabulary) tend to have less difficulty decoding and comprehending. Biemiller (2003) determined that students who enter fourth grade with significant vocabulary deficits show increasing problems with reading even if they have good reading (word identification) skills. Hart & Risley (1995) found that children who begin school lacking vocabulary knowledge can demonstrate a gap of up to seven million words. To close this gap schools need to provide systematic programs of vocabulary instruction throughout the grades (Becker, 1977).

> … students who enter fourth grade with significant vocabulary deficits show increasing problems with reading…

According to Heibert & Kamil (2005), an extensive vocabulary is the bridge between the word-level processes of phonics and the cognitive processes of comprehension. As stated before, an extensive vocabulary is developed over time. On average students learn about 3,000 words a year and by high school graduation know between 25,000 and 40,000 words (Moats, 1999).

What does it mean to "know" a word? To know a word is to have full and flexible knowledge of the word. This knowledge consists of semantic (meaning), syntactic (grammar), morphological (word formation), phonological (sounds or phonemes), orthographical (letter formation), and contextual (implied interpretation based on extended verbal expression) knowledge. In addition to these multiple facets of word knowledge, the average person requires between 12 and 20 encounters with an unknown word before it is known (Stahl, 2003). Hence, on the one hand learning vocabulary is no easy feat, and on the other hand most vocabulary is learned incidentally through environmental exposure.

Needless to say, it is imperative that some vocabulary be taught explicitly; especially vocabulary that represents complex concepts that are not part of a student's everyday experiences (McKeown & Beck, 2004 as cited in Baumann). How do we choose which words to directly teach? Throughout her thirty-year career as a Speech and Language Therapist supporting students with significant vocab-ulary deficits, co-author Mary Ann wrestled with this question. In search of answers she found herself knocking on classroom doors seeking input from grade level and content area teachers, recognizing that collaboration was the key to identifying what academic vocabulary students need to know.

To assist educators in choosing pertinent vocabulary, Beck, McKeown & Kucan (2002) suggest that we consider vocabulary in three tiers (not to be confused with the tiers in RTI). The <u>first</u> tier of vocabulary consists of the most basic words: sister, home, bed, sky, etc. Words in this tier generally do not require instruction in school. The <u>third</u> tier is comprised of words that are infrequently used and most likely limited to specific domains. Most learners do not utilize these words on a frequent basis, so they are best taught as the need arises. Examples of words that fall into this tier include: coagulate, philatelist, and apogee. The <u>second</u> tier encompasses words that are used frequently and are found across several domain areas. Such words include: typical, appearance, scrutinize, infer and dictate.

We support the practice that direct vocabulary instruction in the classroom should focus on Tier 2 words because they have the most impact on students verbal ability and academic functioning. Research has indicated that students' comprehension will increase by 33 percentile points when vocabulary instruction focuses on specific words important to the content they are reading as opposed to words from high-frequency lists (Stahl & Fairbanks, 1986).

> **Research has indicated that students' comprehension will increase by 33 percentile points when vocabulary instruction focuses on specific words important to the content…**

Intentional vocabulary instruction provides students with many opportunities to learn words. One of the best ways to do this is through explicit, systematic instruction, consisting of student-friendly definitions based on rich, vigorous instruction related to words in text, explanation of relationships between words and finally personal connections for each student. Definitions that are student-friendly characterize the word and how it is typically used while explaining the meaning in everyday language.

Along with student-friendly definitions, students need to be actively engaged with the words in order to internalize them for later use. This can be done through making illustrations of unfamiliar words, activating prior knowledge and using the words in writing activities and word games. Other word learning strategies include dictionary use, morphemic analysis, contextual knowledge, and cognate knowledge (words having the same language root or origin), especially for English-language learners (ELLs). In the end the key to successful acquisition of vocabulary is multiple encounters with words both on a formal and informal (word play) basis.

An effective core reading curriculum includes explicit, systematic vocabulary instruction. When teaching vocabulary it is critical that teachers determine each student's knowledge of decoding. If you have questions about phonics we suggest you go to the previous chapter to review this concept.

During instruction of vocabulary a discerning teacher will recognize when a student is not acquiring new vocabulary and will pursue assessment. To assist, we offer the Cardinal Questions as they relate to vocabulary:

1. **What does the student know** about vocabulary?
   - What vocabulary exists in the student's lexicon?
   - What words does the student know receptively ?
   - What words does the student know expressively?

2. **What does the student do** with vocabulary knowledge?
   - What words does the student use for interpersonal communication?
   - What words does the student use to communicate cognitive academic knowledge?

Once you have assessed the student's vocabulary skills and are ready to begin preparation to provide an intervention, think about the remaining three Cardinal Questions:

3. **How does the student learn?** (see Chapter Two)

4. **How does the student approach or react to an unfamiliar task?** (see Chapter Two)

5. **What will you do with the knowledge gained from answering the previous four questions?**

Armed with this information, the following five techniques will assist you in the instruction of vocabulary:

1. Vocabulary Frames
2. Key Words
3. Affix Mason
4. Name That Picture
5. Vocabulary Rehearsal Sheet

"I know words like "sobriquet," "malaise" and "plutocrat."
And I compare the Shaggs to Wittgenstein—how cool is that?"
—Mr. T Experience, *I Wrote A Book About Rock N Roll*

Vocabulary — 1:
Vocabulary Frames

What it is: A technique for learning vocabulary using a four-frame graphic organizer.

When to use it: To teach vocabulary.

⚠ Prerequisites are the ability to read the words and know how to make personal connections with them.

Benefit: Appeals to visual learning styles and allows students to organize their thinking and relate to words in a personal way.

Materials:
- Word lists
- Copies of the Vocabulary Frame Template, pages 240-242, or 5" x 8" index cards
- An overhead transparency of the Vocabulary Frame
- Tracking Progress Form, page 232
- Vocabulary Probes, pages 201-203

Implementation Steps:

1. Choose vocabulary words from the content area that represent "must learn" concepts, or use words from published grade level lists. See the end of this chapter for suggested grade level resources.

2. Introduce the words/concepts (no more than 8 –10 at a time) and their student-friendly definitions.

Note: Definitions that are student-friendly characterize the word and how it is typically used while explaining the meaning in everyday language.

3. Provide students with Vocabulary Frames or have them draw their own on the index cards.

4. Model how to fill in each of the frames. See example of the word *ogle* on the next page. Write the word in frame #1 and the definition in frame #2.

5. Review what it means to make a personal connection with the word or concept. A personal connection is a way to understand a word by attaching it to an idea or concept that is often unique yet makes sense in a meaningful way. Write a sentence or phrase in frame #3 that represents your personal connection to the word.

6. In frame #4, draw a simple graphic that visually represents the word. Discuss with the students how the information in frames #3 and #4 will help them with vocabulary word meaning and recall.

New word Ogle 1	**Personal connection** Young girls walking on the beach wearing a bikini. 3
Student-friendly definition To stare at boldly 2	**Visual association** 4

7.   Have students complete a vocabulary frame for each word on the list or allow the students to identify the words that will personally prove challenging.

8.   Choose one or two words and ask students to share their personal connections and/or visual associations with the rest of the class. Monitor the students' ability to make relevant, unique and authentic connections to the words. Have them explain the thinking that supported their connection and how it helps them understand the word.

Progress Tracking:
  • Record the students' progress each time the technique is used.
    For example:

Group Tracking Progress — Vocabulary					
Word	Student	Personal connection/thinking	+	-	Comment
thrifty	KK	Buying day-old bread (price comparison)	✓		
thrifty	MA	Not spending enough money		✓	Review
ogle	JT	Stare at the very pretty girl in my math class.	✓		

9. Have students keep the vocabulary frames in a notebook or folder for review and practice. The same words can also be used to develop Vocabulary Rehearsal Sheets, which is described later in this chapter.

Variation: Students can use different information within vocabulary frames based on their personal learning preferences. The samples below illustrate some of the different types of information that can be used in the frames.

Frame 2: Sentence Variation, page 241

New word ogle	Personal connection (draw or write)
Definition To stare at boldly	Write a sentence using the word in the content context. *Why do guys ogle girls?*

Frame 3: Example/Non-Example Variation, page 242

New word ogle	Personal connection (draw or write)
Definition To stare at boldly	Examples: 1. *Flirting looks* 1. *Ignoring* Non-examples:

Curriculum Based Measurement: Vocabulary Probes, pages 201-203.

Sources:

Ellis, E. S. (1994). Integrating content with writing strategy instruction: Part I-Orienting students to organizational devices. *Intervention in School and Clinic, 29*, 169-179.

Ellis, E. (1998). *The framing routine*. Lawrence, KS: Edge Enterprises.

Lenz, B. K., Alley, G. R., Beals, V. C., Schumaker, J. B., & Deshler, D. D. (1981). *Teaching LD adolescents a strategy for interpreting visual aids.* Unpublished manuscript, University of Kansas, Lawrence.

Vocabulary — 2:
Key Vocabulary Game

What it is: A technique to remember vocabulary words and their definitions.

When to use it: When students need to build vocabulary knowledge and meaning.

 A prerequisite is the ability to identify key words in definitions.

Benefit: Students will collaboratively engage in word play while determining key words in vocabulary definitions.

Materials:
- Blank 3" x 5" or 5" x 8" index cards
- 25-30 vocabulary words and definitions
- Vocabulary Probes, pages 201-203

Implementation Steps:

1. Use index cards to prepare a deck of vocabulary cards. On each card write a student-friendly definition in the center, the vocabulary word in the lower left corner and the total number of words in the definition in the lower right corner. For example:

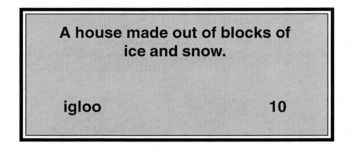

Note: Definitions that are student-friendly characterize the word and how it is typically used while explaining the meaning in every day language.

2. Review the meaning of key words with students prior to the activity. Key words are the most important words in a definition; they provide clues to the meaning of the vocabulary word. For example, in the definition of igloo, the key words would be: house, ice, and blocks. These words provide clues to the identification of the vocabulary word.

3. Divide the class into two, three or four teams. Designate teams by letter A, B, C, or have the teams choose names. The teams can stay together for a predetermined number of games or weeks.

4. A scoring chart similar to the one below is used during the activity to keep track of points awarded while playing the game.

Bombers (A)	Jaguars (B)	X-Team (C)

Playing the Game

1. One student from each team comes to the front of the room. One card is randomly chosen from the deck and the students from each team look at the definition.

2. The student from Team A begins by announcing how many total words are in the definition (e.g., in igloo, the total number of words is 10). The same student continues by choosing a *key word* from the definition and says it aloud to the teams. (e.g., house). The members of Team A confer among themselves to decide on a word and a designated spokesperson provides the answer.

3. If Team A members select the correct word, the team receives the total number of points for the word (if 10 is the number of words in the definition they are awarded 10 points on the scoreboard).

4. If Team A is incorrect, the player from the next team (B) chooses and states a second key word from the definition (e.g., ice). Team B members now confer to determine the correct word and the spokesperson from B answers. If Team B is correct they are awarded one point less than the total number of words in the definition (i.e., if 10 is the total, than nine points are awarded). If Team B is incorrect, play continues rotating through the teams as they identify other key words until the vocabulary word is identified. Each time another key word is selected, the number of points decreases by one.

5. Once the correct word is identified the first round ends and points are awarded to the winning team. New students from the respective teams select a new vocabulary card and play begins again. Rotate the team that starts at the beginning of each round. If teams are unable to identify the vocabulary word once all the words in the definition are provided, no points are awarded.

6. The game ends when all the cards have been used or the designated time ends. Games can be played over several days depending on the number of vocabulary cards. The team with the most points is declared the winner.

Bombers (A)	Jaguars (B)	X-Team (C)
7	9	12
6	11	
	8	

7. Develop new vocabulary word cards and decks throughout the year and incorporate the old cards randomly for cumulative review.

Variation: Another scoring option includes using the vocabulary word in a sentence before awarding any points. If the team is unable to generate an appropriate sentence, play goes to the next team.

Curriculum Based Measurement: Vocabulary Probes, pages 201-203.

Sources:

Scott, J. A., & Nagy, W. E. (1997). Understanding the definitions of unfamiliar verbs. *Reading Research Quarterly, 32(2),* 184-200.

Brett, A., Rothlein, L., and Hurley, M. (1996). Vocabulary acquisition from listening to stories and explanations of target words. *The Elementary School Journal, 96(4),* 415-22.

Vocabulary — 3:
Affix Mason

What it is: A technique for building vocabulary word knowledge utilizing word parts (affixes).

When to use it: When readers do not know how to identify affixes (prefixes and suffixes) and their meanings.

Benefit: Students will be able to build and decode words using affixes.

⚠ Prerequisites are the ability to read the base/root words and divide words into syllables.

📋 *Note: Did you know that affixes are the key to unlocking 14,000 words? That four prefixes will unlock 58 percent of them and four suffixes will unlock 65 percent of them? Additionally, 20 prefixes account for 97 percent of prefixed words in printed school English.*

Materials:
- Blank 3" x 5" or 5" x 8" index cards
- 8 large cards identifying the most common affixes
- Markers, paper, pencils, pens
- Teacher Key Planning Form, page 230
- Tracking Progress Form, page 232
- Vocabulary Probes, pages 201-203

Implementation Steps:
Explain to students that they are going to become Affix Masons. Masons are people who build things using bricks, and they will build words using affixes. Attached before or after a root or base word, an affix is defined as a morpheme or meaningful part of a word that can change the meaning of the word. Affixes include both prefixes and suffixes.

Part 1: Identifying the Four Most Common Prefixes
1. Tell students they will start building words with prefixes. Define prefix as a small but meaningful group of letters that is attached

to the beginning of a base or root word that most often changes the meaning of the word and sometimes changes the grammar.

2. Explain that there are many different prefixes but this activity will only focus on four that change the meaning of a word. Show students the prefix cards *un, dis, re* and *in* with their corresponding meanings. Have the students create their own set of cards and line them up in front of them.

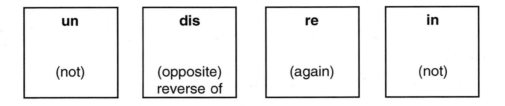

un	dis	re	in
(not)	(opposite) reverse of	(again)	(not)

3. Check the students' ability to read each prefix and then use the process of teach/prompt/test while students respond in unison.
    T: This prefix is *Un. Un* means Not.
    T: Everyone, what does *Un* mean?
    S: Not.
    T: Tell me another way to say *Un.*
    S: Not.

4. Continue with this format until all the prefixes have been introduced. Then, mix up the cards and continue checking for understanding by asking, "What is another way to say _____ ?" When students are firm with the meanings, have them put the cards away and test their prefix knowledge, first as a group and then individually.

5. Create a list of base/root words known to the students, with the first prefix added. Use these words to build a deck of cards by writing the word on one side of the card and the prefix meaning and the base/root word on the reverse side.

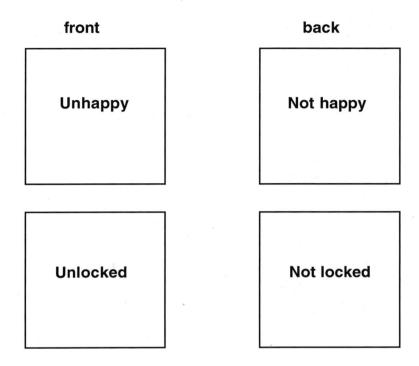

front	**back**
Unhappy	Not happy
Unlocked	Not locked

Planning:

    • Use the Teacher Key to create your plans for this activity. For example:

Teacher Key for Vocabulary

Technique # 3 - Affix Mason

"Listen as I read these words. Identify the meaning of the prefix, combined with the base/root word."

      Sample _un_:

        1.   unhappy
        2.   unlocked
        3.   unfair
        4.   unable
        5.   unzip
        6.   unprepared
        7.   uninterested
        8.   unreal
        9.   undressed
      10.   unusual

---

6. Have the students read the words aloud and identify the meaning of the prefix combined with the base/root word. For example:

    T: The word is unhappy. What is the prefix and what does the word mean?

    S: *Un*, not happy.

    T: What is another way to say not happy?

    S: Unhappy.

7. Next, challenge the students to identify synonyms (words that mean almost the same thing) for each of the words on the cards (i.e., unhappy means not happy or sad or gloomy, or melancholy, etc.). As students generate synonyms write each one on a new index card to use later in word games such as Go Fish, Concentration, etc.

8. Repeat Steps 5 - 7 with the other three prefixes, introducing one at a time. Examples for teaching the other prefixes are as follows: Disappear means opposite of appear; redo means do again; invisible means not visible; etc.

un words	*dis* words	*re* words	*in* words
unhappy	disappear	redo	invisible
uncomfortable	disagree	retake	inactive
unzipped	dishonest	rewrite	incomplete

Progress Tracking:
  • Record the students' progress each time the technique is used.
    For example:

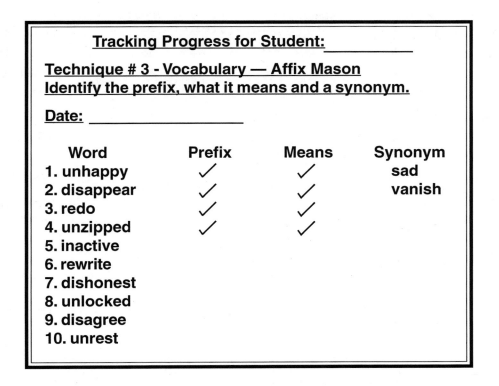

Tracking Progress for Student: _____

Technique # 3 - Vocabulary — Affix Mason
Identify the prefix, what it means and a synonym.

Date: _____

Word	Prefix	Means	Synonym
1. unhappy	✓	✓	sad
2. disappear	✓	✓	vanish
3. redo	✓	✓	
4. unzipped	✓	✓	
5. inactive			
6. rewrite			
7. dishonest			
8. unlocked			
9. disagree			
10. unrest			

Note: Use the chart below to teach additional prefixes and their meanings.

Twenty Most Common Prefixes (* most often used)

un* – not	**pre** – before
re* – again, back	**inter** – between, among
dis* – opposite, reverse of	**fore** – before
in, im, il, ir* – not	**de** – from, reverse
en, em – make, into, in	**trans** – across, over
non – not	**super** – above
in, im – in	**semi** – half
over – too much	**anti** – against
mis – wrong	**mid** – between
sub – under	**under** – under

Part II: Identifying the Four Most Common Suffixes

1. Define suffix as a small but meaningful group of letters that is attached to the end of a base or root word that most often change the grammar of the word but can also change the meaning of the word.

2. Explain that there are many different suffixes but that this activity will only focus on four (*s/es, ing, ed, ly*) Show students the suffix cards *s/es*, *ing*, *ed* and *ly* with their corresponding meanings. Have the students create their own set of cards and line them up in front of them.

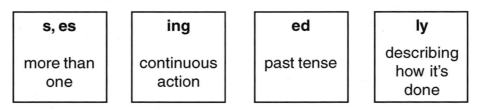

| **s, es**

more than one | **ing**

continuous action | **ed**

past tense | **ly**
describing how it's done |

3. Repeat Part I, Steps 3-8 with suffixes.

Note: Use the chart below to teach additional suffixes and their meaning.

Twenty Most Common Suffixes (* most often used)

-ing* continuous action	**-less** without
-s, -es* more than one	**-able,-ible** can be
-ed* past tense	**-y** characterized by
-ly* describing how it's done	**-er,-est** comparative
-er one who	**-ful** full of
-ic having characteristics of	**-ion,-tion** act, process
-ity,-ty state of	**-en** made of
-ment action or process	**-ness** state of, condition of

-ous, -eous, -ious possessing the qualities of
-ation, ition adjective form of a noun
-ive, -ative, -itive adjective form of a noun
-al,-ial having characteristics of

Curriculum Based Measurement: Vocabulary Probes, pages 201-203.

Sources:
White, T.G., Sowell, J., & Yanagihara, A. (1989). Teaching elementary students to use word-part clues. *The Reading Teacher, 42*, 302-309.

Wysocki, K., & Jenkins, J.R. (1987). Deriving word meanings through morphological generalization. *Reading Research Quarterly, 22*, 66-81.

Vocabulary — 4:
Name That Picture

What it is: A technique to assist students with vocabulary acquisition.

When to use it: To assess and build the students' vocabulary knowledge (personal lexicons).

 Prerequisites are the abilities to attend, listen, and communicate.

Benefit: Students will acquire new vocabulary.

Materials:
- Pictures
- Sticky pads
- Pencils, pens, fine tip markers
- Tracking Progress Forms, pages 231-232
- Vocabulary Probe, pages 201-203

Implementation Steps:

1. Select a picture that represents a content area or a topic taught in your classroom.

2. Explain to the students that together (with their help) you are going to talk about and label everything they see in the picture. Write on sticky notes the vocabulary words that they use to describe the picture. Place the notes on the appropriate parts of the picture. Everyone will have an opportunity to share the words they think of to describe what they see.

3. Begin by giving the students silent time to look at the picture and think about what words they would use to describe what they see. Decide the length of silent time based on the students' ability to sit and observe.

4. At the end of the silent time ask the students what words they would use to label what they see in the picture. As you write the words on the sticky notes, spell them out loud (this is a great opportunity to think aloud, modeling phonological awareness and phonics skills) and then place the sticky note where it is appropriate on the picture.

5. Informally assess the students by urging them to identify everything they perceive.

6. If necessary, scaffold their responses by asking questions and encouraging conversation related to: *who* or *what, size, color, number, shape,* and *action* aspects of the picture.

7. As you continue, elicit more sophisticated vocabulary from your students by evoking words that depict: *mood, location, surroundings, perspective, time, aroma,* and *sound.* Initially you will have to explain some of the more abstract concepts such as mood and perspective.

8. Be sure that any vocabulary you want students to learn is included.

9. Review all the vocabulary words generated and categorize words that share commonalities. Select the words deemed most appropriate to describe the picture through whole class agreement or consensus.

10. Have the students write sentences about the picture using the selected words.

11. Challenge the students to relate the words to something in their own lives, personal connections, that will help them remember the meanings.

12. Finally, ask the students to "Name that Picture" by using no more than four words. Relate this to giving a title to stories, books, movies, and songs.

🗣 Variation 1: Have students work in pairs or small groups using the same picture to create the sticky notes. Each pair or small group then shares their selected words with the class as they place them on the picture. Compare word similarities and differences between groups.

🗣 Variation 2: Have each student create their own set of vocabulary word cards using blank 3" X 5" cards. These cards can be used for teaching and supporting the learning of other skills (i.e., phonological awareness, phonics, antonyms, synonyms, parts of speech).

Progress Tracking:
  • Record the students' progress each time the technique is used.
    For example:

Tracking Progress for Student: *John Doe*

__Technique # 4 -__ **Vocabulary — Using the words in sentences. Score a + if the word is used correctly in a sentence.**

__Date:__ _____

Sample A:
1. _____
2. _____
3. _____
4. _____
5. _____
6. _____
7. _____
8. _____
9. _____
10. _____

_____ % Correct

Curriculum Based Measurement: Vocabulary Probes, pages 201-203.

Source:
Calhoun, E., Poirier, T., Simon, N., Mueller, L. (2001). Three inquiries into the picture word inductive model. Teacher (and District) Research Reports Retrieved from www.nsdc.org/library/publications/jsd/calhoun201.

Vocabulary — 5:
Vocabulary Rehearsal Sheets

What it is: A technique to provide multiple exposures to vocabulary words.

When to use it: After explicit instruction of 8-10 vocabulary words using student-friendly definitions.

 Prerequisites are the ability to read the words and the definitions.

Benefit: Assists students in remembering words and their definitions.

Materials:
- Groups of 8 -10 key vocabulary words and definitions
- Timer
- Rehearsal Sheet Template, page 243
- Vocabulary Probes, pages 201-203

Implementation Steps:

1. Develop a rehearsal sheet for each group of words using the template provided or by creating a Word document table with the use of your computer. To construct the first sheet, randomly fill in the template with one group of 8-10 words so each word appears three to five times on the completed sheet. On a second sheet, write the student-friendly definitions for the words in the exact order of the first sheet. For example:

Note: Definitions that are student-friendly characterize the word and how it is typically used while explaining the meaning in every day language.

Example 1 — Words from the novel *To Kill A Mockingbird*

Rehearsal sheet side 1

Comply	Bewildered	Ingenuous	Moseyin'	Verge	Arbitrated
Diversion	Verge	Bewildered	Ingenuous	Comply	Moseyin'

Rehearsal sheet side 2

To respond to a request	Very confused	Open, honest or naive	To move along	An action that is about to occur	To settle a matter or dispute
Something that distracts the mind	An action that is about to occur	Very confused	Open, honest or naive	To respond to a request	To move along

Example 2 — Words from a science lesson on rocks and minerals

Rehearsal sheet side 1

Igneous Rock	Magma	Inorganic	Sedimentary Rock	Lava	Minerals
Metamorphic Rock	Organic	Lava	Igneous Rock	Magma	Inorganic

Rehearsal sheet side 2

Formed from molten lava "fire rocks"	Molten, hot liquid inside the earth	Non-living	Formed from years of weight and pressure on sediment	Molten, hot liquid outside the earth	Natural, inorganic substances with the same chemical make-up
Formed by rocks that have changed due to heat and pressure	Living	Molten, hot liquid outside the earth	Formed from molten lava, "fire rocks"	Molten, hot liquid inside the earth	Non-living

2. Repeat this process for the other groups of words.

3. Duplicate enough of each sheet to accommodate half of the class. Staple the words and corresponding definition sheets back to back or place in sheet protectors so the words can be viewed on one side and the definitions on the other.

4. Pair up the students. Students can choose their own partners or you can pair them randomly. Explain the rehearsal process.
    a. Identify partner A & B in each pair.
    b. Student A is to look at the definition while student B is looking at the word on the other side of the card.
    c. Explain that you will set a timer for a designated period of time. We suggest no more than one or two minutes.
    d. When you give the signal, student A begins reading the first definition at a partner-audible level and then gives the word (answer). Student B provides feedback by either acknowledging the answer is correct or, if incorrect, immediately telling student A the correct word. Student A continues to read the definitions in a left to right progression row by row, going back to the top if time permits.
    e. Change roles at the end of the designated time and repeat c through d.

Note: Corrective feedback should occur throughout the rehearsal process so that students practice correct answers.

5. Rehearsal sheet #1 is used repeatedly until a new group of words is introduced. To avoid memorization of word order, direct students to start on a different row each time they rehearse.

6. After the new group of words is introduced give the students the second rehearsal sheet. Extend the designated time to 3 or 4 minutes per student. First have them rehearse the new words from sheet # 2 and then return to sheet #1 if time permits for cumulative review.

7. Introduce rehearsal sheet #3 when appropriate and extend the rehearsal time to 4 or 5 minutes per student. Have them rehearse #3 first and return to the previous sheets for review.

8. Continue to develop rehearsal sheets relevant to new vocabulary. Provide rehearsal opportunities for all sheets throughout the year.

Curriculum Based Measurement: Vocabulary Probes, pages 201-203.

Sources:

Stump, C.S., Lovitt,T.C., Fister, S., Kemp, K., Moore, R., Schroeder, B. (1992). Vocabulary intervention for secondary-level youth. *Learning Disability Quarterly*, 15(3), 207-222.

Stahl, S. A. (2003). Words are learned incrementally over multiple exposures. *American Educator, 27(1),* 18-19, 44.

Suggested Resources for Vocabulary

Allen, J. (1999). *Words, Words, Words: Teaching Vocabulary in Grades 3-12.* Portland, ME: Stenhouse.

Bauman, J. F. & Kame'enui, E. J. (editors). (2003). *Vocabulary Instruction: Research to Practice.* New York, NY: The Guilford Press.

Beck, I. (2002). *Bringing Words to Life: Robust Vocabulary Instruction*. New York, NY: The Guilford Press.

Bell, N. (1991). *Visualizing and Verbalizing for Language Comprehension and Thinking.* San Luis Obispo, CA: Lindamood-Bell Learning Processes.

Birsh, J. R. (2005). *Multisensory Teaching of Basic Language Skills 2nd edition.* Baltimore, MD: Paul H. Brooks.

Calhoun, E. (1999). *Teaching Beginning Reading and Writing with the Picture Word Inductive Model.* Alexandria, VA: Association for Supervision and Curriculum and Development.

Carnine, D. W., et al. (2005). Teaching Struggling and At-Risk Readers, *A Direct Instruction Approach*. Upper Saddle River, NJ: Pearson.

Fister, S. L. & Kemp, K. A. (1995). *TGIF: But What Will I Do On Monday.* Longmont, CO: Sopris West Educational Services.

Marzano, R. J. & Pickering, D. J. (2005). *Building Academic Vocabulary Teacher's Manual.* Alexandria, VA: Association for Supervision and Curriculum Development.

Paynter, D., Bodrova, E. & Doty, J. K. (2005). *For the Love of Words: Vocabulary Instruction that Works.* Indianapolis, IN: Jossey-Bass.

Strategic Instruction Model (SIM)
Donald Deschler and Jeanne Schumaker
Center for Research on Learning (CRL)
University of Kansas

The Academic Word List
Averill Coxhead
School of Linguistics & Applied Language Studies
Victoria University of Wellington, New Zealand

Classroom Performance Assessment Appendix C (Grade Level Vocabulary) (2003)
Wayne Secord and Elizabeth Wiig
AZ: Red Rock Educational Publications, Inc.

National Reading Vocabulary
ReadingKey.com/TampaReads.com

Vaughn Gross Center for Reading and Language Arts
http://www.texasreading.org

Florida Center for Reading Research, Student Centered Activities
http://www.fcrr.org

Chapter 9
About Text Comprehension

"They read all the books, but they can't find the answers."
—John Mayer, *No Such Thing*

Text comprehension is the reason for reading. It is what allows us to make sense of what we are reading. When we comprehend we make connections among the ideas in the text and then make connections between the text and our own background knowledge. As we do this we gain new knowledge and we link this new knowledge with what we already know, which promulgates new thoughts. "Once thought of as a natural result of decoding plus oral language, comprehension is now thought of as a much more complex process involving knowledge, experience, thinking, and teaching" (Fielding & Pearson, 1994).

> **"Once thought of as a natural result of decoding plus oral language, comprehension is now thought of as a much more complex process..."**

The teaching part of the complex process of comprehension is our challenge as educators. Comprehension in the past was about reading and answering questions but we now know this is really testing comprehension. Co-authors Mary Ann and Karen cannot remember being taught how to think about the text they were reading, yet each brings a unique perspective to understanding comprehension.

As a young adult, Karen couldn't get her hands on books fast enough. Trips to the neighborhood library meant checking out the maximum number of books each time. Reading for pleasure was a favorite pastime and Karen was always able to complete and return all the books on time while understanding all that she read. It wasn't until high school that she realized that reading content-area textbooks was more involved then reading for pleasure. She was forced to use various techniques such as making notations in the text to differentiate known facts from unfamiliar ones, and writing questions in the margin so she could have conversations with herself about what the author was trying to say. As a visual learner and organizer, Karen often turned to color-coding and mapping to assist her in connecting the critical concepts. This visualization helped her identify the relationships between ideas and remember them for later application. Fortunately for Karen, she had the ability to recognize what she needed in order to make sense of the information presented, and ultimately understand it. Not all students are metacognitive in this way, which is why she knows that providing strategy instruction is so critical for successful comprehension. This is why many of the techniques she used herself are included in this chapter.

> **Not all students are metacognitive. . . which is why providing strategy instruction is so critical for successful comprehension.**

Meanwhile, Mary Ann had a different experience with reading. Mary Ann loved to read, but didn't have much time to do so. She was too busy assisting her family on their small dairy farm and in her leisure time was very involved with athletics and music. She considered herself a slow reader because it seemed like everyone in her class was finishing the reading assignments long before she finished hers. Consequently, Mary Ann became one of those students who developed the skill of faking it in school. She learned that if you paid attention in class the teacher would tell you everything you needed to know for the test. She knew that Cliff's Notes told you the most important things you needed to know about the great novels that were assigned. And fortunately for her, she was able to memorize a great deal of what she read.

However, Mary Ann was not good at summarizing. She was not successful at those workbooks that were supposed to help you learn to choose the best answer that conveyed the main idea of a passage. She despised those assignments, but she just kept doing them because that was the assignment and she loved school. When she went off to college she watched her roommates high-lighting their reading assignments and thought "What a great idea!" She followed suit and ended up with entire pages of text highlighted in brilliant yellow. Obviously she was still unable to distinguish the important information in the text.

Then one day she started making notes and drawing pictures (icons) such as question marks, exclamation points, and light bulbs in the margins to highlight key points in the text, and in the margins of her notes from lectures. At long last, by her sophomore year in college, she had learned to text code on her own. Today, a voracious reader, she continues to develop this skill and wants to share what she has learned.

> **Block and Pressley (2002) stated that comprehension involves more than 30 cognitive and metacognitive processes.**

The complexity of comprehension is illustrated in the work of Block and Pressley (2002) who state that comprehension involves more than 30 cognitive and metacognitive processes. These processes include: clarifying, summarizing, inferencing, and predicting, etc. In addition to the myriad of processes, Willingham (2007) identified and confirmed the following factors as being important for reading comprehension: decoding, fluency and background knowledge. The integration of these factors is critical, with decoding at the helm. If a student can't decode words fluently that student's cognitive energies are concentrated on sounding out the words and there is little or no energy left for connecting to background knowledge and thinking, thus impairing comprehension (Pressley, 2001). It makes sense that if mastering the code is only one aspect of learning to read, then we need to teach the other aspect of learning to read which is how to make sense of the words on the page. We support reading research findings that indicate teaching text comprehension should be emphasized from the beginning of reading instruction. We need to demonstrate that reading is a process of making sense out of text and making connections.

Early instruction in comprehension is conducted orally. Students should be exposed to questioning techniques, self-talk and identifying key ideas before, during and after reading. As students become fluent readers teaching explicit comprehension strategies can

> **Comprehension instruction is a complex and long-term commitment.**

help them *understand* what they read, *remember* what they read, and *utilize* what they read. Comprehension instruction is a complex and long-term commitment that requires teachers to describe, model and guide students in employing strategies while reading text in a variety of content areas. This is why all teachers, regardless of grade level or content area, need to consider themselves "teachers of reading." Educators need to build a common language related to text comprehension across all grade levels and students need to apply comprehension strategies in all subject areas in order to cultivate this critical skill.

The interventions presented in this chapter focus on the most common comprehension techniques for finding the main idea, activating prior knowledge, asking questions, summarizing, visualizing and self-monitoring. As mentioned earlier, we know that we need to begin teaching comprehension strategies in the early years. We also know that to apply comprehension strategies while reading independently students must be able to decode words accurately and fluently, reading at least 50-70 words per minute (Lovitt & Hansen, 1976; Burns et al., 2002), and know their meaning. If you still have questions about fluency we suggest you go to the previous chapter to review this concept; then assess and teach your students accordingly.

During instruction of comprehension a discerning teacher will recognize when a student does not comprehend text and will pursue assessment. To assist, we offer the Cardinal Questions as they relate to comprehension:

1. **What does the student know** about text comprehension?
   - What does the student know about thinking while reading?
   - What does the student know about making connections between the words on the page and his background knowledge?

2. **What does the student do** while demonstrating he comprehends what he has read?
   - Does the student answer questions that are "right there in the text"?
   - Does the student answer "think and search questions"?
   - Does the student answer "on my own questions"?
   - Does the student visualize while reading?
   - Does the student connect text to personal background knowledge?
   - Does the student connect one text to another?
   - Does the student connect text to knowledge of the world?
   - Does the student question the author?

- Does the student generate questions related to what he is reading?
- Does the student summarize text?
- Does the student state the main idea?
- Does the student think of new ideas as a result of his reading?
- Does the student have a sense of wonder or curiosity about what he is reading?

Once you have assessed the student's comprehension skills and you are ready to begin preparation to provide an intervention, think about the remaining three Cardinal Questions:

3. **How does the student learn?** (See Chapter Two)

4. **How does the student approach or react to an unfamiliar task?** (See Chapter Two)

5. **What will you do with the knowledge gained from answering the previous four questions?**

Armed with this information, the following five techniques will assist you in the instruction of comprehension:

1. Making Sense of Reading
2. Passage Essence
3. Think Ahead/Wrap It Up
4. Topic Chart
5. Apprentice Artist

*"And once in a moment, it all comes to you.
As soon as you get it, you want something new."*
—The Cars, *It's All I Can Do*

Text Comprehension — 1: Making Sense of Reading

What it is: A technique to self-monitor using symbols while reading.

When to use it: When students do not think about what they are reading.

⚠️ Prerequisites are the abilities to read fluently and understand most of the vocabulary in the text.

Benefit: Students will become metacognitive (think about their own thinking) while reading.

Materials:
- Copies of subject area texts for students
- Overhead transparencies of the subject area texts
- Transparency pen
- Copies of Making Sense of Reading Bookmarks, page 244
- Comprehension Retell Probe, pages 204-206

Implementation Steps:
1. Explain to the students that you will be demonstrating how to self-monitor while reading text. Have the students brainstorm techniques for making sense of information while reading. Write down all ideas.

2. Define self-monitoring as a continuous internal monologue (self-talk) that occurs during the reading process. Explain the benefits of self-monitoring as they relate to comprehension. Self-monitoring involves:
   1) Questioning unknown ideas, words or concepts
   2) Answering questions
   3) Identifying personal connections
   4) Commenting on information
   5) Thinking about the author's intent

   Discuss each of these benefits and elicit other ideas from the students.

3. Show the students the symbols or notations you will use during the self-monitoring process. A system such as INSERT (Interactive Notation System for Effective Reading and Thinking), (Vaughn & Estes, 1986) can be used or you can develop your own. Explain that a notation system entails marking text with symbols to indicate agreement, importance, novelty or understanding of the information being read. These notations are intended to cue the reader to engage in higher levels of cognition while reading the text and can prove valuable when reviewing the material.

Note: If implementing this technique with other colleagues, across grade levels or school-wide, we strongly suggest using the same symbol/notation system for consistency and effectiveness.

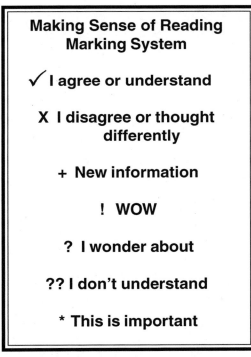

Making Sense of Reading Marking System

✓ **I agree or understand**

X I disagree or thought differently

+ New information

! WOW

? I wonder about

?? I don't understand

* This is important

Adapted from Vaughn and Estes

4. Use one of the transparencies to demonstrate the Making Sense of Reading process. Make your thoughts visible to the student as you engage in your internal monologue while reading. Some examples of visible thoughts include: I can't read this word; I don't know what this word means; Wow, this is interesting; This seems

important; This doesn't make sense; I'm confused; This is new to me, etc.

Note: *Visible thinking is new terminology being used to describe saying/talking aloud your thoughts as you model what you are teaching.*

5. Discuss with the students what they observed during your reading and how the self-monitoring improved your comprehension of the information.

6. Distribute to students a subject area passage and the Making Sense of Reading Bookmark. Use a transparency of the same text to demonstrate the strategy again. This time guide the students through the process step by step.

7. Practice the strategy with the students over several days using both expository and narrative texts until they mark their own text independently.

Note: *Self-monitoring is one of the essential skills for comprehending text. Incorporating self-monitoring into students' repertoire is difficult unless repeated exposure and multiple practice opportunities are provided.*

8. Check students' understanding of the strategy by having them self-monitor during an assigned reading activity. (If students are not permitted to write in their book, provide them with sticky notes so they can make notations on the stickies and apply them to the book pages.) Collect the book or article from the students and award points or a grade for using the process, completing the assignment, and summarizing the information.

Curriculum Based Measurement: Comprehension Retell Probe, pages 204-206

Sources:
Baumann, J. F., Seifert-Kessell, N. & Jones, L. A. (1992). Effect of think-aloud instruction on elementary students' comprehension monitoring abilities. *Journal of Reading Behavior, 24,* 143-172.

Davey, B. (1983). Think aloud: Modeling the cognitive processes of reading comprehension. *Journal of Reading, 27,* 44-47.

Baker, L., & Brown, A.L. (1984). Metacognitive skills and reading. In P.D. Pearson, R. Barr, M.L. Kamil, & P. Mosenthal (Eds.), *Handbook of reading research* (pp. 353-394). White Plains, NY: Longman.

Text Comprehension — 2: Passage Essence

What it is: A technique that equips students with a formula to determine the main idea or essence of a passage (adapted from Collaborative strategic reading).

When to use it: When students exhibit difficulty paraphrasing or summarizing information after reading.

⚠️ Prerequisites for this intervention are the ability to read fluently.

Benefit: Assists students in comprehending the essential information in text.

Materials:
- Highlighters or pens of different colors
- Transparency pens of different colors
- Copies of subject area texts for students
- Overhead transparencies of the subject area texts and T-chart
- Copies of Passage Essence T-charts for students, page 247
- Copies of Passage Essence Bookmark for students, page 246
- Tracking Progress Forms, pages 231-232
- Comprehension Retell Probe, pages 204-206

Implementation Steps:
1. Explain "Passage Essence" as a comprehension strategy used to determine the main idea in a passage.

2. Use the analogy of a book or movie review to explain the benefit of the strategy. A review is a short statement that summarizes a book or movie. Similar to a book or movie review, the essence (main idea) of a passage provides the most important information about the passage.

3. Utilizing the transparencies of the text and T-chart, model how to use the strategy by following the steps below:

Steps to "Passage Essence"
a. Read aloud one passage of selected text.
b. Read the selected text a second time and use a transparency pen to underline/highlight every **who** or **what** in the passage.
c. Using the Passage Essence T-chart transparency, list every **who** or **what** in the appropriate column.
d. Review the **who** or **what** column entries and determine the primary **who** or **what** of this reading selection.
e. Read the selected text a third time and underline/highlight the **most important thing(s) about** the **who or** the **what** in a different color.
f. List the **most important thing(s) about** the who or what in the appropriate column on the T-Chart.
g. Synthesize (find similarities combine) the **most important things about** the who or what and record in the designated column on the T-Chart.
h. Using the **who** or **what** and the synthesized **most important things,** generate the essence of the passage (main idea) in ten words or less. Complete the T-Chart by writing the essence of the passage in the designated area.

Sample passage with important information identified

Key: The **who** or **what** is underlined.
The **most important thing** about the who or what is boxed.

It was a beautiful morning at the lake. The sun cleared the horizon at 4:57 a.m. <u>Mary Ann</u> sprang from <u>her</u> bed as if jumpstarting the brand new day. <u>She</u> had always been an early riser. Today <u>she</u> was going cruising in her 19 Triumph. First, <u>she</u> had to stretch, jog, make coffee and then cut some lilacs for her table. <u>She</u> took off on her daily jog. When <u>she</u> returned and entered her kitchen she noticed the message button blinking on her telephone answering machine. <u>Karen</u> had called and stated that she needed to talk as soon as possible. An urgent message from <u>Karen</u>, <u>Mary Ann</u> wondered? <u>She</u> picked up the phone, found the missed call button and hit send. <u>Her</u> coffee was steaming from her favorite mug when <u>Karen</u> answered. Panic exuded from <u>Karen's</u> voice as she spoke, "Our <u>publishers</u> want the manuscript by midnight."

Example of completed T-chart

Passage Essence T-chart	Student: _____	
Reading selection: _____		
Who or What...	**The most important things about the primary Who or What...**	
Mary Ann	*From the Text*	*Synthesis*
she		
Karen	sprang	fun
publishers	going cruising	exercised
Mary Ann	stretched	
	took off	called Karen
	make coffee	
	cut lilacs	surprised
	hit send	
	wondered	
Primary who or what: Mary Ann		

Essence in ten words or less...

Mary Ann planned a fun day; then the unexpected phone call.

4.   Provide guided practice with a new reading selection. Have students work in pairs or individually.

5.   Compare the "Passage Essence" statements created by students. Discuss similarities and differences between the statements and ask for rationale.

Progress Tracking:
- Record students' progress each time the technique is used. For example:

Group Tracking Progress — Comprehension — Passage Essence					
Student	Passage	Essence of Passage	+	-	Comment
KK	#1	Mary Ann planned a fun day; then the unexpected phone call	✓		
MA	#1	Mary Ann was drinking coffee when she called Karen.		✓	Review
JT	#1	Mary Ann's fun day was interrupted by a surprise phone call.	✓		

6.   Continue with guided practice until students are able to independently generate main ideas in reading assignments.

7.   Have the students use the technique as part of a reading assignment. Collect the T-charts and award credit for using the strategy as well as summarizing and paraphrasing the main idea.

Curriculum Based Measurement: Comprehension Retell Probe, pages 204-206.

Sources:

Klingner, J. K., Vaughn, S. Schumm, J. S. (1998). Collaborative strategic reading during social studies in heterogeneous fourth-grade classrooms. *The Elementary School Journal, 99 (1),* 13-22.

Bryant, D. P., Vaughn, S., Linan-Thompson, S., Ugel, N., Hamff, A., Hougen, M. (2000). Reading outcomes for students with and without reading disabilities in general education middle-school content area classes. *Learning Disability Quarterly, 23 (4),* 238-252.

Text Comprehension — 3: Think Ahead/Wrap It Up

What it is: A before, during and after reading comprehension technique.

When to use it: To establish interest, curiosity and purpose prior to reading, and to review the information after reading.

⚠️ A prerequisite is the ability to generate predictions and meaningful questions related to the text.

Benefit: Students will organize their thoughts about reading and will improve comprehension.

Materials:
- Copies of subject area text for students
- Copies of the Think Ahead Template, page 248
- Copies of Think Ahead Checklist, page 249
- A transparency of the Think Ahead Template and Checklist
- Copies of Think Ahead/Wrap It Up Template (optional), page 250
- Comprehension Retell Probe, pages 204-206

Implementation Steps:

Part I: Think Ahead

1. Define "Think Ahead" as a comprehension strategy used to guide reading and establish a purpose and connection to the text by making predictions and generating questions before reading.

2. Use a movie analogy to explain the benefit of the strategy. Thinking ahead can be likened to viewing a preview of an upcoming movie. The preview is quick yet long enough to make one curious about the movie, forecast what it might be about or ask thoughtful questions before seeing it.

3. Model how to use the strategy using the steps and transparency template below.

Think Ahead Name:	Title/Subject	
Why am I reading this?	What comes to mind?	
	What do I know about it?	
What do I think the reading is about? Predictions 1. 2. 3. 4.	What in the reading supports this?	
What do I want to think about as I am reading? Question 1		
Question 2		
Question 3		
Question 4		
Question 5		

Note: Describe the process while visibly thinking (making your thinking visible to students) and recording your thoughts so that students see and hear each part of the technique.

Steps for "Think Ahead"

1.
    a. Look at the article, chapter, or book (subject area text) and read the title. Write the title/topic on the template.

    b. Think about and ask questions such as: What is my purpose for reading this? Is it for knowledge acquisition or pleasure? What do I think this title/topic is about?

    c. Write down the purpose for reading, what thoughts the title/topic evokes and what you know about the title/topic.

    d. Next, make predictions and write questions about the theme, characters, and outcome (narrative text), or key concepts, definitions, and connecting ideas, etc. (expository text). Explain that the recorded information will be used during and after reading the text.

    e. Read the text aloud while the student follows along. Pause to check off predictions that are true, add pieces of important information and write answers to the questions posed on the Think Ahead Template.

Note: Remind students that the step-by-step process is important to follow while learning the strategy.

2.   Provide guided practice with a new article or chapter. Have students work in pairs or individually while you demonstrate the process again and they complete the template with you. Encourage questioning and clarification throughout the practice.

3.   Give the students a checklist to use during practice and independent work to assist them in following the steps of the process.

Think Ahead Checklist	
1. Did I write my thoughts on title/topic?	✓
2. Did I think about my purpose for reading?	✓
3. Did I write at least 2 or 3 predictions?	
4. Did I write 3-4 questions I want answered from the reading?	
5. Am I ready to read the text?	

Part II: Wrap It Up

1. Once students have mastered the previewing concept, they can advance to the summarizing technique. Staying with the movie analogy, the "Wrap It Up" or summarizing is based on what the movie was about, similar to a movie review.

2. Follow the steps outlined for the previewing technique. This time, use the Think Ahead /Wrap It Template to summarize and determine key points and concepts along with the main idea(s) of the text.

Think Ahead Name:	*Wrap It Up*
Title/Topic:	
What do I know about it? What comes to mind?	Was I right?
Why am I reading this?	How would I rate this?
What do I think the reading is about? Predictions: 1. 2. 3. 4.	What in the reading supports this?
What do I want to think about as I am reading? Question 1:	Answered ?
Question 2:	Answered ?
Question 3:	Answered ?
Summary:	

3. Model how to "Wrap It Up" using the same text that was used for previewing. Use questions such as the following to generate answers and discussion:
   • Did my predictions come true?
   • What parts of the text support my predictions?

- Was I able to answer all my questions? Why or Why not?
- What can I infer or say about the questions or answers?
- Looking back at all the information collected, how can this best be summarized?
- Do I have more questions?
- How would I rate this?
- Would I recommend it to others? Why or why not?

4. Continue with guided practice using a variety of texts until students are able to complete the template independently.

5. Monitor students' abilities to "Think Ahead" and/or "Wrap It Up" by having them independently complete the corresponding template.

6. Use the completed templates to engage students in dialogue about similarities, differences and interpretations of the text.

Currriculum Based Measurement: Comprehension Retell Probe, pages 204-206.

Sources:

Bean, T. W. (1992). Combining text previews and three level study guides to develop critical reading in history. In E. K. Dishner, T. W. Bean, J. E. Readence, & D. B. Moore (Eds.), *Reading in the content areas: Improving classroom instruction* (3rd ed, 264-269), Dubuque, IA: Kendall/Hunt.

Horton, S. V., Lovitt, T. C., & Bergerud, D. (1990). The effectiveness of graphic organizers for three classifications of secondary students in content area classes. *Journal of Learning Disabilities, 23*, 12-22, 29.

Pressley, M., El-Dinary, P.B., Gaskins, I., Schuder, T., Bergman, J., Almasi, L., & Brown, R. (1992). Beyond direct explanation: Transactional instruction of reading comprehension strategies. *Elementary School Journal, 92,* 511-554.

Text Comprehension — 4:
Topic Chart

What it is: A tool to visually chart important ideas and understand the relationships between ideas.

When to use it: Before reading to make predictions, during reading to check for understanding and after reading for comprehension.

⚠️ Prerequisites are the ability to read fluently and differentiate between standard story elements (e.g., character, setting, problem, events, action, solution, outcome etc.).

Benefit: Students can visually and mentally organize critical information from text.

Materials:
- Copies of narrative and expository texts for students
- Copies of the Topic Chart Template, pages 251-252
- Transparencies of the narrative text and Topic Chart
- Transparency pens
- Comprehension Retell Probe, pages 204-206

Implementation Steps:
1. Tell the students they will be completing a Topic Chart which is a way to organize story elements graphically to illustrate text. These charts display the important information from text and how it is related and/or connected.

2. Begin with a review by having the students brainstorm and describe story elements. For example:
   a. Characters—people, major or minor roles
   b. Setting—where, when, period of time
   c. Goals/Problems—plot set-up, issues that occur
   d. Events/Episodes—steps and progress of the plot
   e. Resolution /Outcome—solving the problem(s) in plot
   f. Theme—why the topic matters, (the "so what" as it relates to the reader personally or the universe at large).

Note: For students who require scaffolding, you may want to arrange the elements in the order in which they will occur and then have the students generate questions related to each element. This information can serve as a guide for students while they read the text. Questions can be written next to the elements or directly on the Topic Chart Template.

Example of Elements and Questions

Topic/Title:	
Elements	**Questions**
Characters	**Who are they?** **What are their roles (major or minor)?**
Setting	**Where does it take place?** **Details about the setting.**
Events	**What do the characters do?** **What happens to them?**
Problems	**Is there one or more?**
Resolution	**How does the problem get solved?**

3. Tell students that there are standard elements that can be used to create topic charts.

4. Using the transparency of the narrative text and the topic chart demonstrate how to complete the chart. Show them the topic/ title of the text and write it in the center of the chart (add author if narrative text). Explain that you will complete the remaining boxes as you read the text.

5. Start reading the text aloud and when you come to the first piece of information related to one of the elements, underline it in the text. Show the students where to place it on the topic chart.

6. Continue in this manner, adding the information related to each element until the chart is completed. For example:

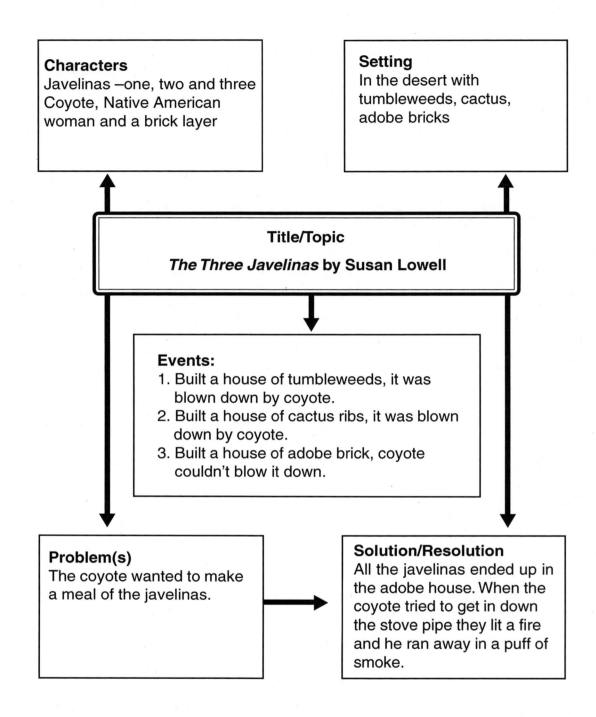

Characters
Javelinas –one, two and three Coyote, Native American woman and a brick layer

Setting
In the desert with tumbleweeds, cactus, adobe bricks

Title/Topic

The Three Javelinas by Susan Lowell

Events:
1. Built a house of tumbleweeds, it was blown down by coyote.
2. Built a house of cactus ribs, it was blown down by coyote.
3. Built a house of adobe brick, coyote couldn't blow it down.

Problem(s)
The coyote wanted to make a meal of the javelinas.

Solution/Resolution
All the javelinas ended up in the adobe house. When the coyote tried to get in down the stove pipe they lit a fire and he ran away in a puff of smoke.

7. Discuss the completed topic chart with the students. Point out how the elements of the topic chart highlight the important information of the text and are related or connected.

8. Demonstrate how to retell the story using the completed topic chart.

9.   Distribute copies of the Topic Chart and a new passage or story to the students. Have the students work in pairs or individually while you demonstrate the process again and they complete the Topic Chart with you. Encourage questioning throughout this guided practice.

10.   Monitor students' ability to complete a Topic Chart by having them complete one independently. Once students demonstrate this ability, facilitate a dialogue to compare charts and discuss similarities and differences. Have students brainstorm uses for the topic charts (i.e., review, study tool, etc.).

Variation 1: Use a similar format to create topic charts or visual notes for other subject areas by relating the standard story elements to information that is found in history, social studies, science and math.

Elements	Social Studies	History	Science	Math
Setting	When and Where	When and Where	Conditions and Time	Problem type
Characters	People or Things	Key players, places & issues	Equipment used	Method, Process or Formula
Problem or Goal	Issues, Troubles to overcome, Contributions	Issues, Purpose, Predicaments	Hypothesis to prove or dispute.	Single or multiple step sequence
Events	Unique features, Commonalities, Areas of interest	Timelines, Dates, Causes, Effects, Turning Points	Steps or process, Chain of events	Steps, Process, Equations
Outcome or Resolution	Results, Current issues	Significance, Impact, Effect	Results, Pros/ Cons Controversy	Final answer Function,
Theme Personal or Universal	Geographic, International, National, Local	Learnings, Links to past & present	Relationship to real life, Significance	Application

Adapted from Raymond Jones, Reading Quest

Variation 2: Have students create their own topic charts. Place the topic in the center of a blank sheet of paper with shapes coming off of the main idea/topic to represent the supporting information. Different-shapes may be used to distinguish types/levels of information.

Curriculum Based Measurement: Comprehension Retell Probe, pages 204-206.

Sources:
Chang, K., Sung, Y. & Chen, I. (2002). The effect of concept mapping to enhance text comprehension and summarization. *Journal of Experimental Education, 71,* 5-23.

Boulineau, T., Fore, C., Hagan-Burke, S. & Burke, M. D. (2004). Use of story-mapping to increase the story-grammar text comprehension of elementary students with learning disabilities. *Learning Disability Quarterly, 24 (2).*

Idol, L. & Croll, V. J. (1987). Story-mapping: Training as a means of improving reading comprehension. *Learning Disability Quarterly, 10 9 (3),* 214-229.

Text Comprehension — 5: Apprentice Artist

What it is: A technique to assist students with visualizing (seeing mental pictures) while reading.

When to use it: When students are unable to create visual images while reading.

Prerequisites are the ability to decode connected text and use drawing utensils and/or a computerized drawing program.

Benefit: Students will acquire the ability to visualize what they read to help with reading comprehension.

Materials:

- 3" x 5" or 5" x 8" index cards with descriptive sentences/passages at each student's independent reading level
- Individual poster cards for these words: *who, what, size, number, color, shape, action, mood, location, surroundings, perspective, time, aroma* and *sound,* displayed prominently in the classroom
- Pencils, pens, fine tip markers, crayons, colored pencils, water colors and/or a computer drawing program
- Blank sheets of paper
- Timer
- Tracking Progress Forms, pages 231-232)
- Comprehension Retell Probe, pages 204-206

Implementation Steps:

Part I: Drawing and Describing a Word

1. Tell students they will become "Apprentice Artists" by drawing pictures of what they see or visualize in their minds while reading.

2. Pass out blank sheets of paper and drawing utensils. Explain to students that they will be drawing a picture of a person, place or thing (a noun). Tell them you will say a word, give them time to think about the word and visualize a picture of what the word portrays. Then they will draw the picture they see in their mind. After they draw the picture they will be describing it.

Note: Present students with words that are familiar nouns (names of people, places or things).

3. For example: "Let's begin… close your eyes so you can you visualize your first picture; the word is, *dog.*" When approximately 30 seconds has passed tell the students to open their eyes and draw their pictures. Allow about two minutes for drawing. When time is up have the students take turns describing their picture so others can visualize it.

4. If students demonstrate difficulty describing their pictures use the words on the poster cards to scaffold their descriptions. Begin by asking questions and eliciting vocabulary related to who or what,

size, number, color, shape and action aspects of their pictures. For more in depth or sophisticated descriptions, require students to depict mood, location, surroundings, perspective, time, aroma and sound. Initially you will have to explain some of the more abstract concepts such as mood and perspective.

Note: The poster word cards, (the "apprentice tools") should be visible in the classroom to be used as reminders of the aspects of creating mental pictures.

5. Record each student's description on the board or on chart paper and then place their pictures near the written description.

6. When everyone has had a turn, discuss how words are used to draw pictures in one's mind. Be sure to mention that this is what authors do *"Create pictures with words."*

7. Have the students compare their pictures and descriptions. Talk about the similarities and differences among pictures. Discuss that similarities and differences based on students' personal experiences and connections.

8. Repeat Steps 1 – 7 with other common nouns to practice visualizing and describing.

9. Repeat Steps 1 – 7 with proper nouns that are familiar to everyone (i.e., Shrek, Harry Potter, Clifford, the Statue of Liberty). Emphasize the similarities among students' words and pictures when they are all visualizing the same person, place or thing.

10. Discuss how authors paint pictures in the reader's mind by evoking images with descriptive words. When the reader understands (comprehends) these words and sees the images, the author's words have come to life for the reader.

Variation 1: Have students work in pairs or small groups, to drawing pictures of people, places, and things. Have them compare their pictures and discuss similarities and differences.

Variation 2: Have students work in pairs and take turns being the speaker/author and listener or apprentice artist. The student speaker/author looks at a picture (without letting the apprentice artist see it) and describes the picture. The apprentice artist then draws the picture that is being described. When they are finished describing and drawing, they compare the pictures and the apprentice artists discuss how the words the speaker/author used helped them create a mental picture.

Part II: Drawing a Sentence/Passage

1. Tell students that the final step to becoming "Apprentice Artists" is to draw a picture based on a sentence/passage they will read.

2. Provide a short descriptive sentence/passage at the appropriate reading level. Have each student read the sentence/passage silently and then allow a reasonable amount of time for the apprentice artists to visualize and draw their pictures.

3. There are different ways to engage students in talking about their pictures. One way is to have all the students display their pictures. Collect all the sentences/passages from the students. Select one sentence/passage and read it aloud. Have students take turns identifying the picture that best represents that sentence/passage. Ask the rest of the students to indicate agreement or disagreement (thumbs up or down response). Discuss why the choice is or is not the best match. Another suggestion for engaging students to talk about their pictures is to display the sentences/passages and collect the pictures. Then hold up a picture and ask students to match the picture to the sentence/passage.

4. Guide the discussion by asking questions and encouraging conversation related to: who or what, size, number, color, shape, and action aspects of the picture. Continue to elicit responses to show how the picture depicts mood, location, surroundings, perspective, time, aroma and sound. Relate these aspects to the sentence/passage.

Note: If students understand inference, this is an excellent opportunity to discuss which of the aspects in the sentence/passage are literal (or right there) and which aspects are left for the reader to imagine, visualize and/or infer.

5.　If any students have been given the same sentence/passage to visualize, have those students compare their pictures, and talk about the similarities and differences and why they exist.

6.　Monitor progress by asking students to read a sentence/passage and draw a picture of what they read.

Progress Tracking:
　• Record students' progress each time the technique is used. For example:

Tracking Progress for Student: _____

Technique # 5 — Comprehension: Apprentice Artist
Record a +/- to indicate whether the picture did or did not match a sentence/passage.

Date(s): October _____

1.	_____	**Sentence A**
2.	_____	**Sentence B**
3.	_____	**Passage A**
4.	_____	
5.	_____	
6.	_____	
7.	_____	
8.	_____	
9.	_____	
10.	_____	

_____ **% Correct**

🗣 Variation 1: Pair up the students. Give each student three to four sentence/passage cards and have them draw pictures to represent their cards. When both students are finished, have the partners exchange the pictures and the cards, then have them match the sentence/passage cards to the pictures and check with their partner for agreement.

🗣 Variation 2: Pair up the students. Have them look at a picture, write a description of what they see and then compare their descriptions.

Curriculum Based Measurement: Comprehension Retell Probe, pages 204-206.

Sources:

Gambrell, L.B., & Bales, R.J. (1986). Mental imagery and the comprehension-monitoring performance of fourth- and fifth-grade poor readers. *Reading Research Quarterly*, *21*, 454-464.

Gambrell, L.B., & Jawitz, P.B. (1993). Mental imagery, text illustrations, and children's story comprehension and recall. *Reading Research Quarterly*, *28*, 264-276.

Pressley, G.M. (1976). Mental imagery helps eight-year-olds remember what they read. *Journal of Educational Psychology*, *68*, 355-359.

Sadoski, M. (1983). An exploratory study of the relationships between reported imagery and the comprehension and recall of a story, *Reading Research Quarterly, 19 (1),* 110-123.

Suggested Resources for Comprehension

Allen, J. (2004). *Tools for Teaching Content Literacy*. Portland, ME: Stenhouse Publishers.

Beers, K. (2002). *When Kids Can't Read: What Teachers Can Do: A Guide for Teachers 6-12*. Portsmouth, NH: Heinemann.

Bell, N. (1991). *Visualizing and Verbalizing for Language Comprehension and Thinking: For Language Comprehension and Thinking.* San Luis Obispo, CA: Lindamood-Bell Learning Processes.

Carnine, D. W., et al. (2005). *Teaching Struggling and At-Risk Readers: A Direct Instruction Approach*. Upper Saddle River, NJ: Prentice Hall.

Deschler, D. & Schumaker, J. *Strategic Instruction Model (SIM).* University of Kansas: Center for Research on Learning (CRL).

Fister, S. & Kemp, K. (1995). *TGIF: Making it Work On Monday.* Longmont, CO: Sopris West.

Gear, A. (2006). *Reading Power: Teaching Students to Think While They Read.* Portland, ME: Stenhouse Publishers.

Harvey, S. & Goudvis, A. (2007). *Strategies That Work: Teaching Comprehension for Understanding and Engagement* .Portland, ME: Stenhouse Publishers.

Klinger, J. K. et al. (2002). *Collaborative Strategic Reading.* Longmont, CO: Sopris West.

Reutzel, D. R. & Cooter, Jr. R. B. (1998). *Balanced Reading Strategies and Practices: Assessing and Assisting Readers with Special Needs*. Upper Saddle River, NJ: Merrill/Prentice Hall.

Tovani, C. (2000). *I Read It, but I Don't Get It: Comprehension Strategies for Adolescent Readers*. Portland, ME: Stenhouse Publishers.

Tovani, C. (2004). *Do I Really Have to Teach Reading?: Content Comprehension, Grades 6-12*. Portland, ME: Stenhouse Publishers.

Wiig, E. H. & Wilson, C. C. (2001). *The Learning Ladder: Assessing and Teaching Text Comprehension*. Greenville, SC: Thinking Publications.

Wiig, E. H. & Wilson, C. C. (2000*). Map It Out: Visual Tools for Thinking, Organizing, and Communicating*. Greenville, SC: Thinking Publications.

Reading Quest Website
Raymond Jones
www.readingquest.org

Vaughn Gross Center for Reading and Language Arts
www.texasreading.org

Florida Center for Reading Research, Student Centered Activities
www.fcrr.org

Chapter 10
About Motivation

"Can't live without passion. Won't live without passion,
Even the president needs passion."
—Rod Stewart, *Passion*

As both authors and practitioners, we are passionate about including **motivation** as a sixth precept to teaching students to read. We believe that unless students are motivated, implementation of any or all of the researched-based, best practices will be in vain. Mary Ann's dad often said, "You can lead a horse to water, but you can't make him drink." She fondly remembers discussions with him about this cliché, often replying, "Dad, the horse will drink when it is thirsty!" We believe that most children enter school "thirsty," with a desire to learn to read (intrinsically motivated). One of our greatest challenges as teachers is determining what to do when learning to read does not come easily. It often becomes the educator's responsibility to inspire students who struggle to stay the course (persistence) and to believe in themselves (self-efficacy). Persistence is a common denominator for both struggling readers and the educators teaching them. How do we instill persistence, self-efficacy and a love of reading? In other words, how do we motivate struggling readers to read?

> **Persistence is a common denominator for both struggling readers and the educators teaching them.**

There are only two true motivators in the world: love and fear. Love and fear are energies that fuel every human thought, word or action. They are the intrinsic motivators. "Fear is the energy which contracts, closes down, draws in, runs, hides, hoards, and harms. Love is the energy which expands, opens up, sends out, stays, reveals, shares, and heals" (Walsch, 1996). Some people identify love and fear as the carrot and the stick. If you contemplate the carrot and the stick you will realize they are external motivators associated with survival, which leads us to ask, is reading really necessary for survival? Wow, now we've opened a can of worms, haven't we?

Society has introduced many extrinsic (external) motivators (rewards)—money, food, etc. Lamentably, our education system sometimes relies only on the extrinsic rewards to inspire students to learn. Think about two of the most common reading rewards (motivators) in many elementary schools across our nation: pizza and ice cream. One can argue that these are effective motivators—kids love pizza and ice cream. Karen remembered how motivated her son was by the pizza incentive, in spite of being a good reader. However, we are aware of no research that supports the effectiveness of pizza or ice cream when it comes to getting struggling readers to read. Not to mention that with the epidemic of childhood obesity, motivating students with food is objectionable.

Success breeds success.

Neuroscientists have determined that the brain makes opiates (drugs used to regulate stress and pain) in the hypothalamus that produce a natural high (Nakamura, 1993 cited in Jensen, 2005). The brain then can be considered a pleasure-seeking system that wants to enjoy positive experiences because those experiences produce a natural high that encourages us to repeat the behaviors. Students who are successful usually feel good and often that's reward enough to keep going. In other words, success breeds success. Thus, the question of how we motivate our students to read must speak to what is happening in their brains while they are learning, or what conditions foster success so that they intrinsically (internal) develop the drive to learn.

Csikszentmihalyi (1990) talks about the concept of *flow*, the psychology of optimal experience. He defines flow as, "the way people describe their state of mind when consciousness is harmoniously ordered, and they want to pursue whatever they are doing for its own sake." Mary Ann interprets it as complete involvement in an experience, which results in that natural high without realizing the passage of time. When we attain flow in our endeavors, we emerge with a sense of accomplishment, growth, satisfaction and the desire to continue or repeat the experience. One of our ultimate goals is to help students achieve flow in their learning. To do so, teachers must think about why they teach. Ask yourself:

- Am I teaching because I love to learn myself?
- Am I teaching because I love the idea of expanding the minds of youth?
- Am I passionate about what I am teaching?
- Do I love to keep searching for new ways to reach students when they do not grasp a concept?
- Do I fear for my students when I realize they are not learning?
- Do I fear for myself if I am not able to teach students in a way that they learn?

Keep in mind the Cardinal Questions and remember the important maxim, "know thyself." Know what motivates you.

All of us have our own stories, our own experiences that shape who we are and what we know. We learned from our parents, our culture and our heritage. Sometimes we learned out of love and sometimes we learned out of fear. So, too, do our students. They arrive at school every morning with one more day of living, one more day of experience and one more day of learning behind them. Each day's experience contributes to students' life stories.

As part of that story, the way in which we fill their days with learning opportunities has a lasting effect on students and their motivation to return to class the next day, ready to learn.

> **… do you inspire in them a reason to read?**

Take time to reflect on the role you play in your students' stories. Ask yourself: Are your students learning something they want to learn? Do they enter the classroom with a love of learning or a fear of what will happen if they do not learn? Do they arrive with apathy or an absence of love? Do they come into the classroom with a sense of wonder? Do you tap into that sense of wonder or squelch it? Do you inspire in them a reason to read?

Let's consider the reasons why students need to learn to read. As we wrote this book we often found ourselves debating this issue. After surveying others, we came up with what we deemed "superficial" reasons (i.e., to achieve better grades, future employment, pleasing others, to get a high school diploma, etc.). These reasons are superficial because there are productive members of society who have compensated for reading deficits and are thriving. Consequently, it appears that reading is not *necessary* for survival.

In addition, the availability of assistive technology (e.g., technology that reads text and writes for you when you speak) gives some people the distorted notion that it's okay if they can't read and write, because the technology will do it for them. It follows then that fear, for some, is not a motivator for learning to read.

So where does that leave us? NCLB demands that educators address illiteracy. Consider activating learning intrinsically by using the motivator known as love—love of learning, love of reading. Instead of asking, "Why do students need to learn to read?" Ask, "Why do students want to learn to read?" The following three personal experiences begin to answer that question.

After listening to a weather forecast predicting significant snowfall, Mary Ann and a friend were discussing what each of them would do if they were housebound for a few days. Mary Ann imagined curling up by the fire with a good book. The friend retorted, "I wish I could do that, but I don't read because reading doesn't hold my attention, so I'll be on the couch watching the tube." Twenty-five hours later, after three feet of ice and snow had fallen and there was a power outage, the two found themselves housebound. Mary Ann curled up by the fire to read. She paused for a moment and wondered what her friend was doing with no television.

> **"I don't read because reading doesn't hold my attention."**

Mary Ann further contemplated what her friend meant when she said, "I don't read because reading doesn't hold my attention." Was this a person who had slipped through the system, who had not been motivated to learn to read, who had not received adequate reading instruction and who would be counted as illiterate in our society? What would have motivated her to be a reader? What would have inspired the persistence needed for this nonreader to become a reader? Is there any way she could have achieved flow while reading?

Another story: Rudy was a student in Karen's ninth grade reading class. He had been in special education and received support as an English language learner since elementary school. Karen, who was in her first year of teaching at the time, was amazed to find out that Rudy was still reading at a primer level. At first she thought he just wasn't motivated to read, as he would put on a display of nonchalance whenever she queried him. He would say things like, "Nobody in my family has ever graduated from high school", "I'm only in high school so I can wrestle" (he did become the state wrestling champion in his weight class as a senior), and "I just can't read all the words, no big deal." After three months of different attempts to teach him to read with very little progress, Rudy finally expressed his true feelings about reading. He really did want to learn to read but he just didn't understand how to put the sounds together. His bravado was simply a mask for the shame he felt because he and other members of his family all had difficulty with reading.

> **His bravado was simply a mask for the shame he felt because he and other members of his family all had difficulty with reading.**

Knowing this, Karen realized the motivation for wanting to read was there. Her job was to find the best approach for teaching to his particular skill deficits. She is happy to report that she found that best way and Rudy not only graduated from high school, but was even able to read the congratulatory words she had written in his yearbook!

Do you remember David? He is the young man in Chapter Five that was excited to finally break the code for reading when he was twenty years old. Mary Ann would be remiss if she did not share the revelation she experienced one day when she was meeting David for lunch at a busy college cafeteria where he was working. Every time they met there for lunch he would order the same food: two slices of cheese pizza and a large soda. Mary Ann assumed this was his favorite food and never questioned the repetitive order. One day, they arrived at the cafeteria early. There were no cafeteria employees or other students around. David sheepishly moved closer to Mary Ann and quietly asked her, "Would you please read the menu to me? I would like to know what else they have to eat here." Stunned, Mary Ann read the menu to David and proceeded to explain the menu items (remember David had a language deficit). Eager to try different foods, he ordered a grilled Italian panini with sweet potato fries on the side. From that day forward when they had lunch together Mary Ann respectfully suggested other menu items to David in a way that did not embarrass him. He was thrilled to try new foods. To this day, Mary Ann reflects on the impact David's inability to read had on his day-to-day living.

The truth is we live in a society that values literacy. We want all students to read so that they have the opportunity to access the many choices available to them. Perhaps one of the most fundamental choices they will need to make will end up being what to do during an extended power outage!

Continue to search for ways to motivate your students so they will want to persist in learning to read. Calvin Coolidge believed,

Nothing in the world takes the place of persistence. Talent will not; nothing is more common than unsuccessful men with great talent. Genius will not; unrewarded genius is almost a proverb. Education will not; the world is full of educated derelicts. Persistence, determination alone is omnipotent. The slogan "Press On" has solved and always will solve the problems of the human race.

"Chug, chug, chug. Puff, puff, puff. Cling-clang, cling-clang. The little train rumbled over the tracks... I think I can, I think I can, I think I can."

The Little Engine That Could by Watty Piper (Platt & Munk Publishing, 1930), is a classic story about believing in one's self (self-efficacy). Teach your students to emulate the little engine and press on. *I will read, I will read, I will read... I can read!*

There are no easy, clear-cut rules for how to motivate students. However, as in earlier chapters, we offer the Cardinal Questions related to motivation as they pertain to you as the educator.

1. **What do you know** about motivation, about motivating yourself, and about motivating others? We think it is critical to reflect on **what you know** and what motivated you to learn it.

2. **What do you do** for work and why? **What do you do** for fun and why?

3. **How do you learn?**
   • What preferences do you have when you learn something new? (See Chapter 2)

4. **How do you approach or react to an unfamiliar task?** In addition to what we present in relationship to this question in Chapter 4, consider the following:
   • What inspires you to approach an unfamiliar task?
   • How do you react when you are presented with an unfamiliar task or challenge that is not your choice?

5. **What will you do with the information you gain from answering the first four questions?** What motivates you to use the information you have gained from answering the first four questions to do something new or different?

A discerning teacher will recognize when a student is not motivated to read and will assess what motivates the student. We offer the following Cardinal Questions with an emphasis on motivation for students.

1. **What does the student know** about motivation?
   • Does the student know about external motivators?
   • What external motivators work for the student?
   • Does the student know about internal motivation?
   • Does the student understand the relationship between internal and external motivation?
   • **What does the student know** and why did he learn it? (A student knows about things he wanted to learn or was motivated to learn.)

2. **What does the student do?**
   • What does the student do outside of school and why?
   • What does the student do in school and why?

3. **How does the student learn?** (See Chapter Two)

4. **How does the student approach or react to an unfamiliar task?** (See Chapter Two)
   • Does the student approach or react to an unfamiliar task differently when he is given a choice?

5.   **What will you do with the knowledge gained from answering the previous four questions?**
     • Consider linking students' interests with what they are reading.

The following five techniques will help you assess what motivates your students:

1.   Getting To Know You
2.   Motivation Noodling
3.   Rank Your Interests
4.   Give Me a Grade Today
5.   Story Chit Chat

"Climb every mountain, search high and low follow every by-way, every path you know."
—Rogers & Hammerstein, *The Sound of Music*

Motivation — 1: Getting to Know You

What it is: An activity for getting to know your students.

When to use it: When you are trying to learn more about your students.

⚠ A prerequisite for teachers is a willingness to take class time to engage students in discussions about topics unrelated to school or the content area.

Benefit: Teachers and students build a safe classroom community of learners.

Materials:
   • Questions challenging students to express attitudes, beliefs, morals, etc.
   • Timer
   • How Motivated Am I? Checklist, pages 209-210

Implementation Steps:

1. Explain that you are interested in getting to know your students and in having them get to know each other and get to know you.

2. Provide class time for students to share their ideas related to thought-provoking questions you provide.

Variation: Once students understand what is considered an appropriate question, have them submit questions for consideration.

3. Allow approximately five minutes at the beginning of each class to ask the question of the day. Sample questions might be:
   - If you could be any place in the world other than here right now, where would you be?
   - If you had a million dollars and could buy only one thing, what would it be?
   - What is your favorite food?
   - If you could have only one thing to eat for a month, what would it be?
   - What is your favorite color?
   - What is your favorite book, TV show, toy, video game, etc.?
   - What is your favorite/least favorite time in school and why?
   - What is your favorite/least favorite time at home and why?

Note: Questions should be specific to age and grade level. Repeat some of the same questions at different times throughout the year to see if students' responses remain the same or change.

4. Have students take turns recording responses. Discuss similarities, common interests and differences among students. Share your own thoughts and answers to the questions.

Note: Extend the discussion or relate to other subject areas by incorporating graphing to create a profile of the responses.

5. Occasionally ask students to write down their answers. Collect answers and use them to establish small groups based on similarities or differences.

6. Reflect on how you might process the information with the students and relate their responses to a particular subject area.

Monitoring:
- How Motivated Am I? Checklist , pages 209-210.

Motivation — 2: Motivation Noodling

What it is: An activity for getting to know your students.

When to use it: When searching for topics or interests to motivate your students to read.

⚠️ Prerequisites for teachers are the skill of observation and a willingness to accept and learn about students' individual differences and interests.

Benefit: Students feel that teachers are taking a personal interest in their passions and life outside of school.

Materials:
- 3" x 5" or 5" x 8" index cards
- How Motivated Am I? Checklist, pages 209-210

Implementation Steps:
1. Become an observer. Take notice of your students in order to make comments or ask questions that are significant to the individual. Look at:
   - T-shirts (i.e., logos depicting artists, music, beliefs)
   - Hairstyles
   - Clothing
   - Backpacks
   - Magazines, books, CDs, notebooks
   - Snacks

2. Begin to "noodle" with your students (Lopate, 1975). Noodling occurs over time (i.e., a quick comment here, a quick comment there, a quick question now, a quick question later). When you "noodle" you comment on and ask about things such as:
   • Music preferences
   • Video games (level of achievement and inherent motivators)
   • Blogging sites (myspace, etc.)

3. As you discover students' interests and who or what inspires them, engage them in conversations related to their interests such as: Who has written about this topic? What did they say? What new ideas does it spark? What do you think about it? What is the opposing view? What are related topics?

4. Teachers and students can brainstorm together to identify resources for exploring answers to these and other questions. Use this opportunity to engage students in reading. What text will the student want to read? What does the teacher need to do to make reading materials accessible to each student? What roadblocks, if any, prohibit the student from accessing the topic information?

5. Keep index cards of the students' interests. Refer to them when giving assignments that allow students to choose how they will demonstrate understanding of a subject area.

Monitoring:
• How Motivated Am I? Checklist, pages 209-210.

Motivation — 3:
Ranking Your Interests

What it is: An activity to get to know your students.

When to use it: When you are looking for topics or interests to motivate your students to read.

⚠ Prerequisites for teachers are a willingness to have students complete the interest survey and to use that information when planning lessons.

Benefit: Students feel that teachers are taking a personal interest in their interests and lives outside of school.

Materials:
- Copies for students of Interest Survey, pages 253-254
- Scissors
- Blank sheets of paper
- Motivation Checklist, pages 209-210

Implementation Steps:
1. Explain to students that you want to know more about their personal interests.

2. Provide class time for students to complete the survey. Present them with the survey and review the directions.

3. Collect the completed rank-ordered surveys. As your peruse them, look for common interests among students. Surveys can be helpful for differentiating instruction and grouping students by similar or different interests.

4. Consider how to connect student interests to your classroom content.

Note: Ask students to complete this Interest Survey at least twice a year. It allows students to share new interests and passions.

Monitoring:
- How Motivated Am I? Checklist, pages 209-210.

Motivation — 4:
Give Me a Grade Today

What it is: An activity for students to summarize what they learned in a class and provide the teacher with feedback regarding the lesson.

When to use it: At the end of a lesson, for students to process their learning and for you to receive feedback about your instruction and determine what the students still need.

 A prerequisite is a willingness to accept feedback from students.

Benefit: Teachers learn about the impact their teaching style has on students and about how well students are able to summarize what they have learned and take responsibility for their learning.

Materials:
- Give Me a Grade Today Template, page 255
- How Motivated Am I? Checklist, pages 209-210

Implementation Steps:
1. Tell students that you are interested in having a conversation about school—both teaching and learning. Explain that you want to know in their own words what they are learning during class and what they still need to learn in order to understand the concept/topic.

2. Introduce and talk about feedback. Point out that feedback can be either positive or negative. Provide positive feedback by complimenting or acknowledging something another person has done. Provide negative feedback when you are concerned about something a person has done and then make a suggestion for how he can do it differently the next time. Positive feedback maintains behavior. In other words, explain that if you do something they like, they should let you know so that you may do it again. Negative feedback changes behavior. If students do not like something you do, they may suggest what you can do differently the next time.

3. Give each student a copy of Give Me a Grade Today Template. Demonstrate how to complete it:
   - First, students summarize what the lesson was about and whether or not it was interesting. Have them brainstorm to create a word bank of vocabulary that can be used to describe degrees of interest (i.e., outstanding, superb, brilliant, boring, repetitive, confusing, etc.);
   - Second, students assign the teacher a grade (A, B, C, etc.) and explain why they gave that grade;
   - Third, explain what the teacher could do differently next time that would be helpful;
   - Fourth, determine and explain what is still needed for them to better understand the topic.

4. At the beginning of this activity, when you decide to use the form, inform students that you will be asking them to give you a grade. Allow time at the end of class for them to complete the form.

5. From time to time, discuss the students' responses especially when you will be making a change as a result of their feedback.

Monitoring:
   - How Motivated Am I? Checklist, page 209-210.

Motivation — 5: Story Chit Chat

What it is: An activity to get to know about your students' background experiences with reading and story telling.

When to use it: When you are trying to learn more about your students' cultures, traditions and practices.

⚠️ A prerequisite for teachers is a willingness to use brief periods of class time to chat about stories.

Benefit: Teachers gain insight into students' feelings about reading and story telling, helping build a community of learners.

Materials:
- Timer
- How Motivated Am I? Checklist, pages 209-210

Implementation Steps:

1. Provide class time for 'chit chat' about reading and story telling. This activity is most beneficial even when used daily for only three to five minutes at the beginning or end of the class.

2. Explain to students that you are interested in learning about their cultures, traditions and practices.

3. Have students take turns talking about their past reading and story telling experiences. Be sensitive to differences (i.e., religious, economic, racial, family structure, etc.).

4. Here are sample openers for story chit chats:

   - A story I remember my _____ telling me is _____ I remember this story because _____
   - A book I remember my _____ reading to me is _____ I liked this book because _____
   - My favorite children's book is_____ because _____
   - I was so embarrassed when _____ asked me to read _____ because _____
   - I was so excited when _____ asked me to read _____ because _____
   - I was so mad when _____ asked me to read _____ because _____
   - I was so sad when _____ asked me to read _____
   - The first book I learned to read was _____ It was about _____

- I liked it when my teacher read _____ because _____
- I liked it when my teacher told the story about _____ because _____
- A book I wish I could read is_____ because _____
- A book I am reading now is_____ I am reading it because _____
- Reading is like _____ because _____

Note: Each story opener activity may need to occur over several days so every student has an opportunity to chit chat about their experience.

5.   Listen for expressions of love and fear when students chit chat. Consider how to incorporate students' feelings into future lessons.

Monitoring:
- How Motivated Am I? Checklist, pages 209-210.

Suggested Resources for Motivation

Blanchard, K. et al. (2002). *Whale Done! The Power of Positive.* New York, NY: Simon & Schuster.

Fister, S. & Kemp, K. (1995). *TGIF: Making it Work On Monday.* Longmont, CO: Sopris West.

Gibbs, J. (2001). *Tribes: A New Way of Learning and Being Together.* Windsor, CA: Center Source Systems.

Harper, K. (1992). *Zapp! In Education.* New York, NY: Ballantine Books.

Johnson, L. (2005). *Teaching Outside the Box: How to Grab Your Students by Their Brains.* Indianapolis, IN: Jossey-Bass.

Lopate, P. (1989). *Being With Children*. New York, NY: Doubleday.

Sullo, B. (2007). *Activating the Desire to Learn.* Alexandria, VA: Association for Supervision and Curriculum Development.

Chapter 11
Next Steps

"It has to start somewhere, it has to start sometime.
What better place than here?
What better time than now?"
—Rage Against the Machine, *Guerilla Radio*

As you address the process of teaching all students to read, we hope this book has stimulated your desire to learn more about the exciting world of literacy including: effective instruction, interventions and measurement of student learning. As mentioned in the introduction, this book is just the tip of the iceberg; there is a vast glacier out there to explore. We encourage you to use the research and the resources mentioned herein to change your way of thinking about teaching all children to read.

One of the best ways to do this is through collaboration with others. Seek out individuals who share your passion. Spend time together brainstorming, discussing and most importantly, challenging each other for the purpose of building knowledge. Don't be surprised when you start saying things like, "That's a great idea, why aren't others using it?" Or, "I'm not sure about this, let's keep talking." Or, "I don't understand, What does that mean?" Perhaps even, "We've got some great stuff here, maybe we should write a book!" Don't laugh—that's exactly how Mary Ann and Karen started. The realization that others share your interests, ideas, and enthusiasm about a cause is the foundation for building powerful relationships, which can lead to amazing results.

> **Seek out individuals who share your passion.**

With high-quality instruction, an appropriate curriculum, interventions that work and collaboration whenever possible, 85-90 percent of students will more than likely experience success. Students who require additional targeted or intensive interventions will benefit most if a planned approach is agreed to by all and implemented with fidelity.

This, of course, requires administrative support from inception. As students experience success at the secondary and tertiary levels of intervention they either continue receiving additional support, return to the core classroom program or are considered for additional intervention. The cohort of students who fail to respond to intensive levels of intervention is generally a very small number, about 5-10 percent. These students should receive full consideration for referral to special education without delay.

> **Students who require additional . . . interventions will benefit most if a planned approach is agreed to by all and implemented with fidelity.**

As part of the referral process, you will be asked to supply all documentation leading up to this decision. This means gathering all the pertinent information collected throughout the RTI process. The Intervention Tracking Form, pages 227-228, and charted data will provide concise yet comprehensive information for review by the Special Education Committee or Multi-Disciplinary Team.

Prior to submitting a referral, take time to review all of your paper-work. Bear in mind a few facts put forth in IDEA 2004, the newly reauthor-ized federal regulations governing students with disabilities. A student cannot be considered for special education if it has been determined that:
1. the student has not received appropriate reading and math instruc-tion as set forth by NCLB, including the five precepts of reading;
2. the student is limited in English proficiency;
3. the student's difficulty is a result of being culturally or economically disadvantaged.

Change these statements into questions and be honest with your response.
- Has the student received high quality, scientifically-based reading instruction since Kindergarten?
- Is the student an English language learner?
- Does the student have a cultural or economic disadvantage?

> **It is important to note that progress monitoring does not stop once an IEP is developed.**

If you can answer yes to the first question and no to the last two with certainty, move forward with the referral, but don't forget to include the documentation that satisfies the first question.

The documented results obtained through progress monitoring at all tiers will provide the evaluation team with a wealth of information. At this point, a classroom observation, social history and physical examination, along with specific area assessments, may be all that is needed to complete a comprehensive evaluation.

If a student is found eligible for academic or behavioral services, then special education becomes the sustained, intensive intervention necessary for the student to access the general education curriculum successfully. Often, this degree of intervention means continuing what was provided at Tier III along with an Individualized Education Program (IEP). It is important to note that progress monitoring does not stop once an IEP is developed. Rather, the monitoring continues on a daily, weekly or monthly basis, using the present levels of performance as the baseline levels and the annual goals as performance aims.

Now that you're here, where do you start? Our suggestion is this: "Think outside the fences that surround your mind."

- Seek out a colleague in your building that you have never worked with before.
- Ask if he/she has read *RTI: The Classroom Connection.*
- No?, "Would you like to borrow my copy?" Oh wait, you probably don't want to give up your copy! So, refer them to National Professional Resources, Inc.
- Yes?, Ask them the first Cardinal Question—"What do you know?"

Collaboration is key, but working outside the proverbial box of traditional roles is cutting edge. We can eliminate the ironclad concept of "your kids" and "my kids" by building professional learning communities that consider creative scheduling, dynamic student grouping and unconventional teaching arrangements. As you begin to break down fences, both real and imaginary, bear in mind this final piece of advice from Karen Kaiser Clark: "Life is change, growth is optional!"

"Gonna change my way of thinking,
make myself a different set of rules.
Gonna put my good foot forward
and stop being influenced by fools."
—Bob Dylan, *Gonna Change My Way Of Thinking*

Appendix A
Curriculum Based Measurement Probes, and their Directions

Within this Appendix is a sample probe, and specific directions for its use, for each of the interventions in this book. The probes can be used to assess the effectiveness of a chosen intervention. They will provide valid information when administered as benchmarks several times during an intervention. In order to conduct continuous progress monitoring, a pool of probes would need to be developed or purchased commercially. Refer to the Resource section of Chapter 4 for a list of commercially available probes.

Curriculum Area		Relates to Chapter
Phonemic Awareness – Segmentation	Directions	5
Phonemic Awareness – Segmentation	Probe	5
Phonics – Sound Fluency	Directions	6
Phonics – Sound Fluency	Probe	6
Phonics – Nonsense and Expanded Words	Directions	6
Phonics – Nonsense Words	Probe	6
Phonics – Expanded Nonsense Words	Probe	6
Fluency – Word Identification	Directions	7
Fluency – Word Identification	Probe	7
Fluency – Oral Reading	Directions	7
Vocabulary – For A & B	Directions	8
Comprehension – Retell	Directions	9
Comprehension – Retell	Template	9
Comprehension – Maze	Directions	9
Motivation – How Motivated Am I?	Directions	10
Motivation – How Motivated Am I?	Checklist	10
Graphing Scores	Directions	5-9
Graphing Charts	Samples	5-9

Phonemic Awareness Segmentation
Probe Directions

The Phonemic Awareness probe that is most relevant is phoneme segmentation fluency. The goal is to have the student segment as many three-, four- and five-phoneme words into their respective phonemes in a one minute time frame. The following is a sample of this probe. It is appropriate to begin this probe in the winter for Kindergartners and continue until the student reaches 35+ in one minute.

Directions:

1.   Have the student sit across from you. Have a stopwatch and clipboard with the words ready to go. Say to the student: "I am going to say a word to you. When I am finished saying it, I want you to tell me all the sounds in the word. Lets practice one. I say "top" you would say /t/ /o/ /p/. Now you do it. Tell me the sounds in "mob."

Correct Response: If the student says /m/ /o/ /b/ you say very good the sounds in mob are /m/ /o/ /b/.

Incorrect Response: If the student gives any other response or no response you say the sounds in "mob" are /m/ /o/ /b/. Your turn what are the sounds in "mob?"

2.   OK. Here is your first word. Begin timing as soon as you finish saying the word. Stop at one minute.

Scoring:

Word	Student Says	Scoring	Correct Segments
brush	"b...r...u...sh"	/b/ /r/ /u/ /sh	4/4
brush	"br...ush"	/br/ /ush/	2/4
brush	"bru...ush"	/bru/ /ush/	2/4
brush	"br...brush"	/br/ /brush/	1/4
brush	"bu...ru...u...sh"	/bu/ /ru/ /u/ /sh/	4/4
brush	"b...r...u...sh...t"	/b/ /r/ /u/ /sh/	4/4
brush	"b...r...u...TH..."	/b/ /r/ /u/ /TH/	4/4
brush	"b...rrrrrr...uuuu...sh"	/b/ /r/ /u/ /sh/	4/4
brush	"b...ush"	/b/ /ush/	2/4
brush	"brush"	/brush/	0/4

3.   If the student does not respond in three seconds after you say a word, score a zero for that word and say the next word. Discontinue this probe if the student says no correct sound segments in the first five words.

Students are not penalized for dialect or articulation errors.

Phonemic Awareness Segmentation Probe

Student:_____ **Given by:** _____ **Date:** _____

shop /sh/ /o/ /p/	wait /w/ /ai/ /t/	___/6 (6)
burn /b/ /ir/ /n/	love /l/ /u/ /v/	___/6 (12)
lamb /l/ /a/ /m/	how /h/ /ow/	___/5 (17)
toes /t/ /oe/ /z/	stop /s/ /t/ /o/ /p/	___/7 (24)
face /f/ /ai/ /s/	girl /g/ /ir/ /l/	___/6 (30)
theme /th/ /ea/ /m/	type /t/ ie/ /p/	___/6 (36)
marks /m/ /ar/ /k/ /s/	adds /a/ /d/ /z/	___/7 (43)
am /a/ /m/	hook /h/ /oo/ /k/	___/5 (48)
walk /w/ /aw/ /k/	hopped /h/ /o/ /p/ /t/	___/7 (55)
brush /b/ /r/ /u/ /sh/	ouch /ow/ /ch/	___/6 (61)
lake /l/ /ae/ /k/	each /ea/ /ch/	___/5 (66)
stops /s/ /t/ /o / /p/ /s/	up /u/ /p/	___/7 (73)
crane /k/ /r/ /ae/ /n/	wires /w//ie/ /r/ /z/	___/8 (81)
		___/___

Kemp & Eaton, 2007

Phonics — Sound Fluency
Probe Directions

Fluency can be applied to letter sounds, words, phrases or connected text. The process for administering each of these probes is similar; however, the scoring varies depending on what is being assessed. In all cases, the probe is 1 minute in length and is administered individually.

Letter-sound probes are administered individually. Sheets are developed with all 26 letters and 3 digraphs. Two copies of each sheet are needed. One for the student and one for the teacher to record corrects and errors. See example.

Student Copy

g	d	n	y	sh
v	j	a	x	s
e	k	p	o	l
h	th	v	m	f
r	c	w	t	ch
i	z	u	b	k
o	x	ch	z	j
th	a	g	c	r

Teacher Copy

g	d	n	y	sh
v	j	a	x	s
e	k	p	o	l
h	th	v	m	f
r	c	w	t	ch
i	z	u	b	k
o	x	ch	z	j
th	a	g	c	r

Directions:

1. Explain to the student that he will be reading the sounds aloud as you point to each letter on the sheet. He should do his best and attempt each item. Ask if there are any questions.

2. Set a timer for one minute out of the student's view. Tell the student to begin and then start the timer when they say the first sound. Each time the student answers correctly, point to the next letter. If the student identifies a sound incorrectly or does not respond within 3 seconds, tell him the sound, draw a line through the letter to indicate an error and move to the next letter. When assessing letter sounds only short vowel sounds are correct responses.

3. At the end of the minute, tell the student to stop and circle the last letter read on your copy. Thank the student for his participation.

4. Count the total number of correct sounds and then count the number of errors. Proficiency is determined based on the following benchmarks.

40-60 sounds per minute

For additional information on proficiency levels see:

DIBELS benchmarks goals
http://dibels.uoregon.edu/benchmarkgoals.pdf

or

AIMSweb norms
http://www.aimsweb.com/measures/literacy/norms.php

Phonics — Sound Fluency
Probe

g	d	n	y	sh
v	j	a	x	s
e	k	p	o	l
h	th	v	m	f
r	c	w	t	ch
i	z	u	b	k
o	x	ch	z	j
th	a	g	c	r

Kemp & Eaton, 2007

Phonics — Nonsense Word (CVC) and Expanded Nonsense Word Fluency Probe Directions

The Phonics measurement that is most relevant is nonsense word fluency. The goal is to have the student decode as many nonsense words as he can in a one minute time frame. It is appropriate to begin the CVC probe in the winter for Kindergarteners and continue until the student reaches 50+ and reads 15 whole words accurately in one minute. It is anticipated that most students will achieve the CVC benchmark by the fall of second grade.

Note: You may want to administer the Expanded Nonsense Fluency Probe once a student has achieved the CVC benchmark to assess his ability to read the six syllable types.

Directions:

Have the student sit across from you. Create two 3" x 5" cards with the practice nonsense words "saz" and "lup". Have a stopwatch and a clipboard with a copy of Nonsense Word Probe ready to go. Say to the student:

"I am going to have you read some pretend or make-believe words today." Show the student the practice word "saz". Look at this word (point to it as you say this). "It is not a real word, it is a make-believe word. Watch and listen to me as I read this word: /s/ /ă/ /z/, "saz" (point to each letter as you say the sound (phoneme) associated with the letter, then run your finger fast beneath the word as you say the word). I can say the sounds of the letters /s/ /ă/ /z/ (point to each letter) or I can say the whole word "saz" (run your finger beneath the word as you say it)."

"Now it is your turn to read a pretend word. Show the student the practice word "lup". Read this word the best you can (point to the word "lup"). Make sure you say any sounds you know."

Correct Response: If the student says /l/ /ŭ/ /p/ all of the sounds, you say "very good the sounds are /l/ /ŭ/ /p/."

Incorrect Response: If the student gives any other response or no response you say "Remember you can say the sounds or you can say the whole word. Listen and watch me: /l/ /ŭ/ /p/ (point to each letter as you say the sound) or "lup" (run your finger beneath the word as you say it). I would like to have you try again. Read this word the best you can (point to the word "lup")."

Place the copy of the student probe in front of the student.

Say to the student: "Here are some more pretend words. Start here (point to the first word) and go across the page (point across the first row on the page). When I say, 'Start,' read the words the best you can. Remember you can point to each letter and tell me the sound that goes with it or you can read the whole word. Read the best you can. Okay, get ready, put your finger on the first word, 'Start'." (Start your timer as soon as you finish saying "Start".

Scoring:

Word	Student Says	Scoring	Correct Segments
lup	"l...u...p"	l u p	3/3
lup	"lup"	lup	3/3
lup	"l...up"	l up	3/3
lup	"loop"	l oo p	2/3
lup	"lub"	lu b	2/3
lup	"l...u...up"	l u up	3/3
lup	"l" (3 seconds)*	l ___	3/3
lup	"pul"**	p u l	1/3
lup	"p...l...u"**	p l u	1/3
lup	"lusp"	l u p	3/3

Discontinue if the student reads no sounds or words correctly in the first five words.

Students are not penalized for dialect or articulation errors.

*Three-Second Rules:
- Sound by sound—if the student is saying individual letter sounds and hesitates for three seconds, score the letter sound incorrect, say the correct letter sound to the student, then point to the next letter and ask, "What sound?"

- Word by word—if the student is reading words and hesitates for three seconds, score no points for the word, say the correct word to the student, then point to the next word and ask, "What word?"

**Sound Order Rules
- Sound by sound—if the student is saying individual letters sound by sound and says the correct sound for the letters but says them out of order, he is given points for the number of letter sound combinations said correctly. You want to give students credit for beginning to learn the letter/sound correspondence (the alphabetic principle).
- Word by word—when the student is saying the whole word (blending the sounds) he must be in the correct order. You may give partial credit for sounds that are said in correct placement.)

ip	baf	huj	lat	sib	ruv	el
mog	vun	ith	hep	cag	kitch	yot
zeth	lish	fet	pim	thip	ped	wum
rud	kak	min	sith	vul	din	lev
cip	dep	kith	zal	ij	ux	gol
shap	viv	lob	mab	nup	fot	huj

Kemp & Eaton, 2007

sote	sheg	lat	doit	rigfap
ped	chab	spoud	mabe	sib
napsate	posh	meest	plofent	zint
clabom	trisk	knap	ig	bave
skree	nup	lunaf	felly	pim
clirt	dreker	chur	bloot	kelm
strone	hedfert	fet	tive	brinbert
dreef	bremick	guddy	dess	pelnador
pate	baf	poth	shratted	frip
depate	crenidmoke	sline	poth	strone

Kemp & Eaton, 2007

Fluency
Word Identification
Probe Directions

The word fluency probe is one minute in length and is administered individually. Development of word fluency should be part of reading instruction until students can read in the range of 60-80 grade level words in isolation a minute.

How it works:

Word fluency probes consist of reading real words to develop speed and accuracy. Two copies of the probes are needed. One for the student and one for the teacher to record corrects and errors. See example of beginning sight word probe.

Student Copy

the	of	he	and	yes
what	this	for	one	red
by	an	other	up	is
book	some	will	like	make
than	me	so	long	find
do	many	your	it	no
these	two	my	find	be
at	day	she	not	each
go	see	out	to	fast
help	been	did	him	or

Teacher Copy

the	of	he	and	yes
what	this	for	one	red
by	an	other	up	is
book	some	will	like	make
than	me	so	long	find
do	many	your	it	no
these	two	my	find	be
at	day	she	not	each
go	see	out	to	fast
help	been	did	him	or

Directions:

1.   Explain to the student that he will be reading words aloud. He should do his best reading and attempt each word. Ask the student if they have any questions.

2.   Set a timer for one minute out of the student's view. Tell the student to begin and then start the timer when they say the first word. Follow along on your copy as the student reads. If the student says a word

incorrectly, draw a line through the word to indicate an error. Do not correct the student but allow him to continue reading. If he hesitates for three seconds, draw a line through the word to indicate an error, and point to the next word.

3.   At the end of the minute, tell the student to stop, circle the last word read on your copy and thank the student for reading.

4.   Count the total number of words read correctly. Record the score on a chart or graph.

the	of	he	and	yes
what	this	for	one	red
by	an	other	up	is
book	some	will	like	make
than	me	so	long	find
do	many	your	it	no
these	two	my	find	be
at	day	she	not	each
go	see	out	to	fast
help	been	did	him	or

Kemp & Eaton, 2007

Fluency—Oral Reading
Probe Directions

Fluency can be applied to letter identification, words, phrases or connected text. If a student reads less than 20 words a minute in a passage consider slicing back to phrase or word fluency. Oral Reading Fluency is 1 minute in length and is administered individually. Development of reading fluency should be part of reading instruction until students can read at least 135 words a minute.

How it works:

Oral reading fluency requires a passage of 150-200 words from grade level material. Two copies of the passage are needed. One for the student and one for the teacher to record corrects and errors. See example.

Student Copy

| Summertime! How lovely it was out |
| in the country, with the wheat |
| standing yellow, the oats green, |
| and the hay all stacked down in the |
| grassy meadows! And there went the |
| stork on his long red legs, |
| chattering away in Egyptian, for he |
| had learnt that language from his |
| mother. The fields and meadows |

Teacher Copy

Summertime! How lovely it was out	6
in the country, with the wheat	12
standing yellow, the oats green,	17
and the hay all stacked down in the	25
grassy meadows! And there went the	31
stork on his long red legs,	37
chattering away in Egyptian, for he	43
had learnt that language from his	49
mother. The fields and meadows	54

Reprinted with permission from Intervention Central

Directions:

1.   Choose a passage that is at the student's grade level. If the student reads with less than 95% accuracy, slice back until the passage is at the independent level of reading. Probes can be created from classroom materials or easily obtained from the suggested resources in Chapter 4.

2.   Explain to the student that he will be reading the passage aloud. He should do his best reading and attempt each word but if he comes to

a word he doesn't know you will tell him what it is and he is to keep reading. Ask the student if he has any questions.

3. Set a timer for one minute out of the student's view. Tell the student to begin and then start the timer when he says the first word. Follow along on your copy of the passage. If the student says a word incorrectly, draw a line through the word to indicate an error. Do not correct the student but allow him to continue reading. If at any time the student hesitates for three seconds, provide him with the word immediately. Do not allow him to sound it out. Any word you provide is indicated on your copy as an error.

4. When the timer rings, tell the student to stop reading. Indicate the ending point on your copy of the passage and thank the student for reading.

5. Count the total number of words read and then count the number of errors. The correctly read words (CRW) is obtained by subtracting the errors from the total words.

Scoring

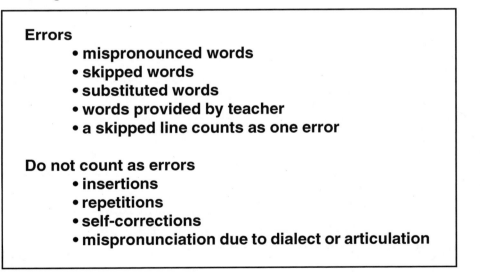

Errors
- mispronounced words
- skipped words
- substituted words
- words provided by teacher
- a skipped line counts as one error

Do not count as errors
- insertions
- repetitions
- self-corrections
- mispronunciation due to dialect or articulation

Summertime! How lovely it was out	6
in the country, with the wheat	12
standing yellow, the oats green,	17
and the hay all stacked down in the	25
grassy meadows! And there went the	31
stork on his long red legs,	37
chattering away in Egyptian, for he	43
had learnt that language from his	49
mother.The fields and meadows	54

Correct word per minute scores can be recorded in the following way and then transferred to a chart for a visual display.

date	1/10	1/14	1/20	1/25	2/4	2/9			
total	50								
errors	5								
CRW	45								

Oral reading rates are not a precise score, but a range that indicates where a typical reader is expected to perform.

Reading rates by grade level	
Level	**Correct Words/minute**
Second half of first grade	50-70
Second grade	90-100
Third grade	100-120
Fourth grade	120-140
Fifth grade and beyond	140 +

Note: This information has been compiled from a variety of sources including: Rasinski, Tindal and Hasbrouck, and Fuchs and Fuchs.

Vocabulary—*Probes A & B*
Directions

Probe A

1. Create a pool of potential vocabulary terms in the identified content area that will be taught over the course of the year. From the pool, choose 35-40 words that represent 4-6 weeks of content material. Use these words to develop one probe.

2. Use the Referral Sheet Template (See Appendix B) or, on your computer, create a table large enough to include **all** of the words. Randomly insert the definitions into the table so each occurs only once on the sheet. The vocabulary words that correspond to the definitions are written in the same order on a separate table for a self-correcting answer key.

3. For the most reliable results, create more than one probe containing the same words placed in a different order.

To respond to a request	Very confused	Open, honest or naïve	To move along	An action that is about to occur	To settle a matter or dispute
_____	_____	_____	_____	_____	_____
Something that distracts the mind					
_____	_____	_____	_____	_____	_____

4. Instruct the students that they will have 3 minutes* to complete the assessment by reading the definitions silently and writing the corresponding word underneath. Explain that they are to complete as many items as they can during the 3 minutes. When they come to a term they do not know or have not yet been taught, they should skip it in order to complete as many items as they can in the allotted time. At the end of the 3 minutes, have students count the number of correct and incorrect answers (blanks are not considered incorrect) then keep track

of the data on a separate sheet. *Students should not be able to finish the probe within the time limit. If this occurs, shorten the time limit. Once established, keep the time and the number of items consistent with every administration of the probe.

5.   Administer the probe weekly until all words included in the probe have been introduced.

6.   Proficiency for vocabulary probes is approximately 20-30 words written per minute. Words that are written in their entirety will take longer than abbreviations. Determine ahead of time how students will be allowed to respond.

7.   Keep track of number of correct words by recording progress on a checklist or a graph.

Probe B

Students can also be assessed using a freestyle response vocabulary probe.

Here are some Vocabulary starters:
- Write or Say words related to a topic:
  Vacation, School, Rocks, Slavery, Civil War etc.
- Write or Say words to describe a picture.
- Write or Say words that are opposites (antonyms) or alike (synonyms).
- Write or Say words that start with the letter_____.
- Write or Say words that describe story characters.

Directions:

1.   Use this type of probe at the beginning at a lesson/unit to find out what students know; and then throughout the unit to find out what students have learned. The probe can be administered to the entire group if the responses are written or you can administer it individually by having the student say the words aloud. The probes are administered for a pre-determined amount of time, usually one minute. Proficiency is 20-30 words in a minute.

2. Tell the students they will freestyle write or say the words for 1 minute. At the end of the minute tell students to stop.

3. Scoring of the probe can occur in several ways. You can choose students to read their words and the other students can check to see if the have those words on their list. Students can query to see if a word they have written is correct. Words that do not meet the topic criteria are incorrect. You can also have students count the words they wrote, write that number on the paper and turn the paper in to you. Score by counting 1 for a correct response and count the total number of responses. Once scored return the papers and have students record their scores on a chart or graph.

4. After the next administration, score probes again. Count correct responses and have students compare to their previous score to see if improvement has occurred.

Comprehension—Retell
Directions

The comprehension skill most frequently used in daily living is summarizing information in one's own words. Proficiency in this area is 20-30 correct pieces of information in a minute, with 2 or fewer incorrect responses (Starlin, 1982).

How it works:

1. Choose text that is written at the student's instructional level and is at least 600-800 words in length for readers at 4th grade level or above. It may be necessary to assess the student's oral reading fluency first to ensure readability of the passage. Have a Comprehension Retell template available to record the student's responses. Indicate the student's name, the date of the first probe and the passage reading level.

2. Explain to the student that they will read a passage silently for three minutes and then tell you everything they remember (facts, ideas, concepts, main idea, interpretations etc.) from the reading in their own words (summarize). The student will have one minute to summarize.

    Note: If the student is a fluent reader and reads the entire passage, you may want to increase the retell time to 2 minutes the next time the probe is administered. Remember to keep the reading time and the retell time consistent thereafter.

Directions:

1. Provide the student with the appropriate reading passage and ask him to begin reading. Start the timing. At the end of three minutes ask them to stop reading.

2. Using the retell template, ask the student to tell you everything he remembers about the passage by summarizing the information in his own words. For each element or piece of information that is correct, put a tally mark in the corresponding column. If the student stops during the minute timeframe, prompt him by saying, "What else do you remember?"

3. Keep track of the time and at the end of the minute stop marking the template. Allow the student to continue if he is in the middle of a thought or comment.

4. Use the information obtained from the retell summary to determine what elements the student can recall and what areas require additional intervention.

Comprehension—Retell
Template

Elements Make a mark for each idea or fact	Date	Date	Date	Date	Date
Title or Author					
Character names: Who?					
Character details – What?					
Setting: When, Where?					
Setting details – What?					
Events – Sequence?					
Event details					
Infers					
Draws conclusions					
Gives opinions					
Makes personal connections					
Interprets					
Identifies main idea					
Total					
Comments:					

Kemp & Eaton, 2007

Comprehension — Maze Comprehension
Directions

What it is:

Mazes are composed of a variety of passages with mixed genres and styles.

How to develop:

The passages begin with a complete sentence. For every remaining sentence, the 7th word is replaced with a word choice. The word choice is composed of 3 words: one correct and 2 distracters. Distracters must be within one letter in length of the correct choice and only one replacement is semantically correct.

- Put correct choices and distracters in bold, separated by a forward slash, and underlined.
- Keep the maze selections intact rather than splitting at the end of lines
- Create passages that are long enough so students will not finish in the allotted time
- If the seventh word is a proper noun, move one word forward or back
- Vary the placement of the correct maze choice
- If the 7th word is the first word in the sentence, capitalize correct choice and distracters (Fuchs and Fuchs, 1992). See example below.

Vitamin D Lowers Risk Of Cancer

Vitamin D cut the risk of several types of cancer by 60% overall for older women in the most rigorous study yet. The new research strengthens the case (**mark/miss/made**) by some specialists that vitamin D (**may/was/let**) be a powerful cancer preventative and most (**figures/people/nurses**) should get more of it. Experts (**remain/domain /totals**) split, though, on how much to make/take/. The findings are a breakthrough of (great/heart/ medical and public health importance.

How it works:

Choose passages that are at the student's current grade level. It may be necessary to assess oral reading fluency first to ensure readability of the passage. If a student is well below grade level expectations, he or she may need to read from a lower grade level passage.

1.   Maze comprehension can be administered in a group setting.

2.   **Tell** students they will have 2.5 minutes to read the passage to themselves and circle the correct word for each blank. The examiner monitors the students during the 2.5 minutes and scores each test later.

3.   **Scoring**—When the student makes 3 consecutive errors, scoring is discontinued (no subsequent correct replacement is counted). Skipped blanks (with no circles) are counted as errors. The score is the number of correct replacements circled in 2.5 minutes.

4th grade – 20 correct in 2.5 minutes
5th grade – 25 correct in 2.5 minutes
6th grade – 30 correct in 2.5 minutes

Note: Maze comprehension probes can be obtained from a variety of sources. See Chapter 4 About CBM for ordering information.

Motivation—How Motivated Am I?
Directions (for Checklist)

Use this checklist at the end of a class as often as you would like to have students report about their effort.

Directions:

Give each student their own copy of How Motivated Am I? Review the directions and demonstrate how to fill in the columns. Ask students to be honest because you are looking for feedback from them.

Today's Date	6/9											
1. How hard did I try?	3											
2. How much did I follow the teacher's directions?	2											
3. How much did I like this topic?	0											
Total Points	5											

Motivation—How Motivated Am I? Checklist

Name:_____ Class: _____

How Motivated Am I?

Directions: Write today's date in the appropriate column. Then answer the three questions about your effort for today's class using the following point system: **Not at all = 0   A little bit = 1   Some = 3   A lot = 4**

Today's Date											
1. How hard did I try?											
2. How much did I follow the teacher's directions?											
3. How much did I like this topic?											
Total Points											

Today's Date											
1. How hard did I try?											
2. How much did I follow the teacher's directions?											
3. How much did I like this topic?											
Total Points											

Today's Date											
1. How hard did I try?											
2. How much did I follow the teacher's directions?											
3. How much did I like this topic?											
Total Points											

Kemp & Eaton, 2007

Graphing Scores

After collecting data from the curriculum based measure, you will want to graph the student scores to obtain a visual representation of their progress. This is a vital aspect of the assessment. Graphing provides a picture of the student's progress and assists in the decision making process of instruction that is working or needs to be changed. The data on a chart can easily be shared with other staff, parents and the student.

There are two options for creating graphs for individual students in the classroom. The first option is to create your own charts using graph paper or pre-made templates (see pages 212-215). The second option is to use Excel spreadsheets, purchase graphing software (see Chapter 4) or use graphing websites that allow you to input the data and then generate charts for you.

Here are three excellent graphing websites:

1. http://easycbm.com
2. www.oswego.edu/~mcdougal or www.acsedge.com/norms/index/html
3. www.kasp.org/ToolsandResources

Note: If you create your own charts, be sure the vertical axis of the graph accommodates the highest range of scores of all students in the class. For example, oral reading fluency scores can range from 0 to over 200, whereas, retell comprehension fluency doesn't need to exceed 50. The horizontal axis represents the weeks of instruction and it is best to indicate the exact date the probe was administered for progress tracking.

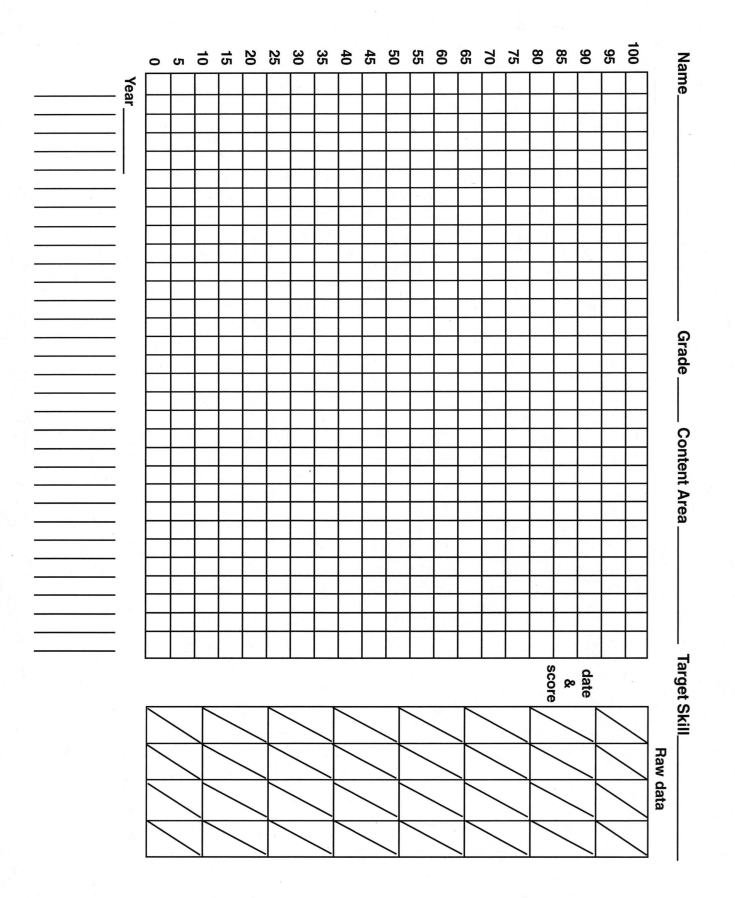

Name _____ Grade _____ Content Area _____ Target Skill _____

Year _____

100
95
90
85
80
75
70
65
60
55
50
45
40
35
30
25
20
15
10
5
0

date & score

Raw data

Name_____ **Grade**_____
Content Area _____ **Target Skill**_____

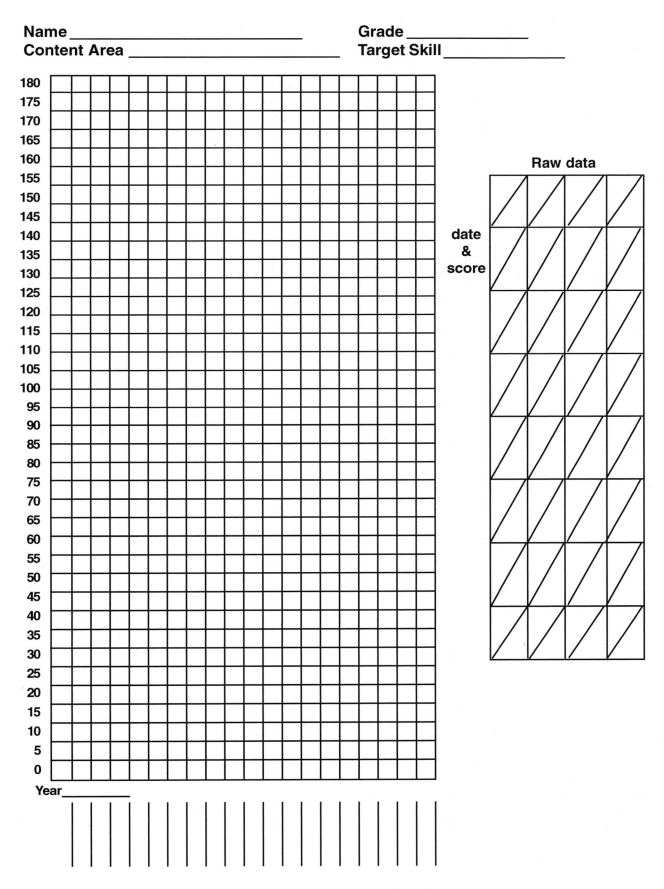

Name _____   **Grade** _____

Content Area _____   **Target Skill** _____

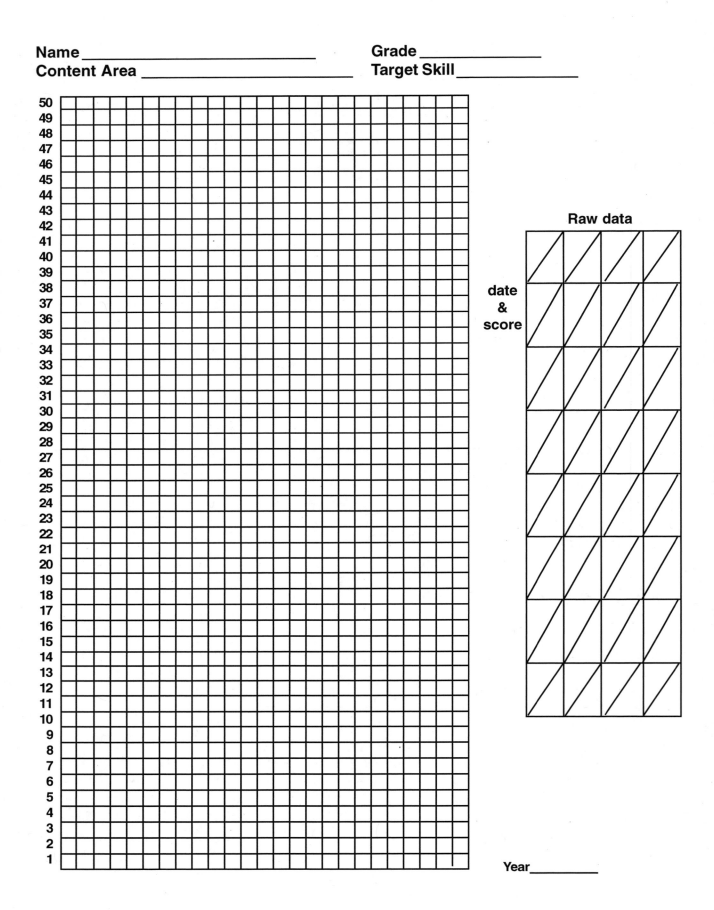

Raw data

date
&
score

Year_____

Name _____ **Grade** _____

Content Area _____ **Target Skill** _____

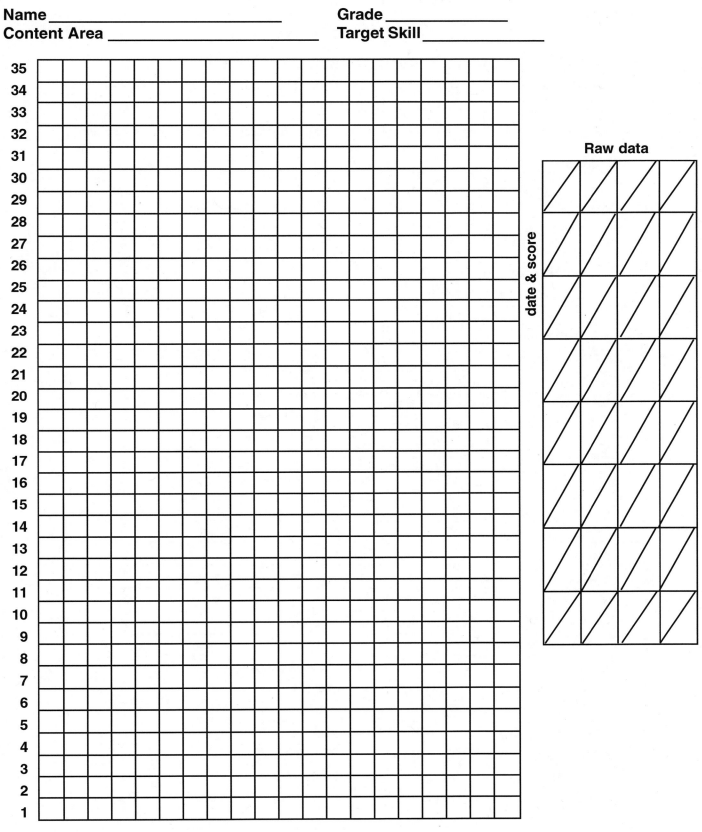

Year_____

Appendix B
Reproducibles

Within this Appendix are a variety of reproducible forms and materials that will enhance the implementation of interventions provided in this book. For ease of use, the chapter to which they are associated is cited.

Reproducibles	Relates to Chapter
Cardinal Questions for Educators	2
Cardinal Questions for Students – One Set for Each of the Five Areas, plus Motivation	2
Response To Intervention Planning Document	3
Intervention Tracking Form	3
Teacher Key Planning Form	5-9
Individual Tracking Progress Form	5-9
Group Tracking Progress Form	5-9
44 Phonemes of Standard American English	5-6
Phonics – Six Syllable Types (1 & 2)	6
Phonics – Six Syllable Types (3 & 4)	6
Phonics – Six Syllable Types (5 & 6)	6
Fluency – Fluency Feedback Form	7
Fluency – Oral Reading Fluency Scale	7
Fluency – Data Collection Sheet	7
Fluency – Graphing Chart	7
Vocabulary – Frame 1, Visual Association	8
Vocabulary – Frame 2, Sentence Variation	8
Vocabulary – Frame 3, Example & Non-Example Variations	8
Vocabulary – Rehearsal Sheet Template	8
Comprehension – Making Sense of Reading Bookmarks	9
Comprehension – Passage Essence Steps	9
Comprehension – Passage Essence Bookmarks	9
Comprehension – Passage Essence T-chart	9
Comprehension – Think Ahead Template	9
Comprehension – Think Ahead Checklist	9
Comprehension – Think Ahead/Wrap It Up Template	9
Comprehension – Topic Chart Template	9
Comprehension – Topic Chart Template with Questions	9
Motivation – Interest Survey	10
Motivation – Give Me A Grade Today Template	10

Cardinal Questions for Educators

1. **What do you know** about your content area - in this case, about culturally responsive, research based reading instruction? In other words, **what do you know** about teaching reading and its five component skills—phonemic awareness, phonics, fluency, vocabulary and comprehension plus motivation?

2. **What do you do** about meeting the learning needs of all your students? In this case, **what do you do** about meeting the learning needs of your students while teaching reading?

3. **How do you learn?** To meet your optimal learning needs:
    • What environmental preferences do you have (i.e. noise, lighting, chairs, workspace, temperature)?
    • What is your preferred sensory input modality (i.e. visual, auditory, motor)?
    • How are you smart (i.e. logic smart, music smart, body smart, picture smart, word smart, people smart, self smart, nature smart)?

4. **How do you approach or react to an unfamiliar task?** When you learn something new, how are you affected by
    • Your cognitive style (i.e. impulsive/reflective, global/particular, leveler/ sharpener, synthetic/analytic, inductive/deductive, concrete/abstract, random/sequential)?
    • Your personality type (i.e. introvert/extrovert, sensory-intuitive, thinking-feeling, judging-perceiving)?
    • Your motivation to learn (i.e. intrinsic, extrinsic)?

5. **What will you do with the information you gain from answering the first four questions?**

Motivation Cardinal Questions for Educators

1. **What do you know** about motivation, about motivating yourself, and about motivating others**?** We think it is critical to reflect on **what do you know** and what motivated you to learn it?

2. **What do you do** for work and why**? What do you do** for fun and why?

3. How do you learn?
   • What preferences do you have when you learn something new? (See Chapter 2)

4. **How do you approach or react to an unfamiliar task?** In addition to what we present in relationship to this question in Chapter 4 consider the following:
   • What inspires you to approach an unfamiliar task?
   • How do you react when you are presented with an unfamiliar task or challenge that is not your choice?

5. **What will you do with the information you gain from answering the first four questions?** What motivates you to use the information you have gained from answering the first four questions to do something new or different?

Cardinal Questions for Students
Phonemic Awareness

1.   **What does the student know** about oral language and phonemic awareness?
     • What is the student's first language?
     • How would you describe the student's oral language?

2.   **What does the student do** when asked to demonstrate oral language skills?
     • Does the student articulate the 44+ phonemes of Standard American English?
     • Does the student rhyme?
     • Does the student discriminate between same and different phonemes?
     • Does the student blend phonemes to form words?
     • Does the student segment words into phonemes?

3.   **How does the student learn?** To meet the student's optimal learning needs:
     • What are the student's environmental preferences (i.e. noise, lighting, chairs, workspace, temperature)?
     • What is the student's preferred sensory input modality (i.e. visual, auditory, motor)?
     • How is the student smart (i.e. logic smart, music smart, body smart, picture smart, word smart, people smart, self smart, nature smart)?

4.   **How does the student approach or react to an unfamiliar task?** When the student is learning something new, how are their behaviors affected by
     • their cognitive style (i.e. impulsive/reflective, global/particular, leveler/ sharpener, synthetic/analytic, inductive/deductive, concrete/abstract, random/sequential)?
     • their personality type (i.e. introvert/extrovert, sensory-intuitive, thinking-feeling, judging-perceiving)?
     • their motivation to learn (i.e. intrinsic, extrinsic)?

5.   **What will you do with the knowledge gained from answering the previous four questions?**

Cardinal Questions for Students
Phonics

1. **What does the student know** about phonics?
   - What does the student know about the 26 letters of Standard American English?
   - What does the student know about linking letters and sounds?
   - What does the student know about breaking words into syllables?

2. **What does the student do** when asked to read unfamiliar words?
   - What phonemes (sounds) does the student connect (map) to graphemes (letters) in isolation? *This is decoding or sounding out at the single phoneme level.*
   - What graphemes (letters) does the student map to phonemes (sounds) in isolation? *This is encoding or spelling at the single phoneme level.*
   - What one syllable nonsense or pseudo-words does the student sound out (decode)?
   - What one syllable nonsense or pseudo-words does the student spell (encode)?
   - What does the student do when asked to decode (read) multi-syllabic words?

3. **How does the student learn?** To meet the student's optimal learning needs:
   - What are the student's environmental preferences (i.e. noise, lighting, chairs, workspace, temperature)?
   - What is the student's preferred sensory input modality (i.e. visual, auditory, motor)?
   - How is the student smart (i.e. logic smart, music smart, body smart, picture smart, word smart, people smart, self smart, nature smart)?

4. **How does the student approach or react to an unfamiliar task?** When the student is learning something new, how are their behaviors affected by
   - their cognitive style (i.e. impulsive/reflective, global/particular, leveler/sharpener, synthetic/analytic, inductive/deductive, concrete/abstract, random/sequential)?

- their personality type (i.e. introvert/extrovert, sensory-intuitive, thinking-feeling, judging-perceiving)?
- their motivation to learn (i.e. intrinsic, extrinsic)?

5. **What will you do with the knowledge gained from answering the previous four questions?**

Cardinal Questions for Students
Fluency

1. **What does the student know** about fluency?
   - **What does the student know** about reading aloud fluently?
   - **What does the student know** about reading with expression?
   - **What does the student know** about reading connected text at a conversational rate?

2. **What does the student do** when asked to read aloud?
   - How many words correct per minute (WCPM) does the student read?
   - What is the student's independent reading level?
   - Does the student read with appropriate prosody?
   - Does the student decode connected text instantaneously?

3. **How does the student learn?** To meet the student's optimal learning needs:
   - What are the student's environmental preferences (i.e. noise, lighting, chairs, workspace, temperature)?
   - What is the student's preferred sensory input modality (i.e. visual, auditory, motor)?
   - How is the student smart (i.e. logic smart, music smart, body smart, picture smart, word smart, people smart, self smart, nature smart)?

4. **How does the student approach or react to an unfamiliar task?** When the student is learning something new, how are their behaviors affected by
   - their cognitive style (i.e. impulsive/reflective, global/particular, leveler/ sharpener, synthetic/analytic, inductive/deductive, concrete/abstract, random/sequential)?
   - their personality type (i.e. introvert/extrovert, sensory-intuitive, thinking-feeling, judging-perceiving)?
   - their motivation to learn (i.e. intrinsic, extrinsic)?

5. **What will you do with the knowledge gained from answering the previous four questions?**

Cardinal Questions for Students
Vocabulary

1. **What does the student know** about vocabulary?
   - What vocabulary exists in this student's lexicon?
   - What words does this student know receptively ?
   - What words does this student know expressively?

2. **What does the student do** with vocabulary knowledge?
   - What words does this student use for interpersonal communication?
   - What words does this student use to communicate cognitive academic knowledge?

3. **How does the student learn?** To meet the student's optimal learning needs:
   - What are the student's environmental preferences (i.e. noise, lighting, chairs, workspace, temperature)?
   - What is the student's preferred sensory input modality (i.e. visual, auditory, motor)?
   - How is the student smart (i.e. logic smart, music smart, body smart, picture smart, word smart, people smart, self smart, nature smart)?

4. **How does the student approach or react to an unfamiliar task?** When the student is learning something new, how are their behaviors affected by
   - their cognitive style (i.e. impulsive/reflective, global/particular, leveler/sharpener, synthetic/analytic, inductive/deductive, concrete/abstract, random/sequential)?
   - their personality type (i.e. introvert/extrovert, sensory-intuitive, thinking-feeling, judging-perceiving)?
   - their motivation to learn (i.e. intrinsic, extrinsic)?

5. **What will you do with the knowledge gained from answering the previous four questions?**

Cardinal Questions for Students
Comprehension

1. **What does the student know** about text comprehension?
   - What does the student know about thinking while reading?
   - What does the student know about making connections between the words on the page and their background knowledge?

2. **What does the student do** while demonstrating they comprehend what they have read?
   - Does the student answer questions that are "right there in the text"?
   - Does the student answer "think and search questions"?
   - Does the student answer "on my own questions"?
   - Does the student visualize while reading?
   - Does the student connect text to personal background knowledge?
   - Does the student connect this text to other text?
   - Does the student connect text to knowledge of the world?
   - Does the student question the author?
   - Does the student generate questions related to what they are reading?
   - Does the student summarize text?
   - Does the student state the main idea?
   - Does the student think of new ideas as a result of their reading?
   - Does the student have a sense of wonder or curiosity about what they are reading?

3. **How does the student learn?** To meet the student's optimal learning needs:
   - What are the student's environmental preferences (i.e. noise, lighting, chairs, workspace, temperature)?
   - What is the student's preferred sensory input modality (i.e. visual, auditory, motor)?
   - How is the student smart (i.e. logic smart, music smart, body smart, picture smart, word smart, people smart, self smart, nature smart)?

4. **How does the student approach or react to an unfamiliar task?**
   When the student is learning something new, how are their behaviors affected by
   - their cognitive style (i.e. impulsive/reflective, global/particular, leveler/ sharpener, synthetic/analytic, inductive/deductive, concrete/abstract, random/sequential)?
   - their personality type (i.e. introvert/extrovert, sensory-intuitive, thinking-feeling, judging-perceiving)?
   - their motivation to learn (i.e. intrinsic, extrinsic)?

5. **What will you do with the knowledge gained from answering the previous four questions?**

Cardinal Questions for Students
Motivation

1. **What does the student know** about motivation**?**
   - Does the student know about external motivators?
   - What external motivators work for the student?
   - Does the student know about internal motivation?
   - Does the student understand the relationship between internal and external motivation?
   - **What does the student know** and why did they learn it? (A student knows about things they wanted to learn or were motivated to learn.)

2. **What does the student do?**
   - What does the student do outside of school and why?
   - What does the student do in school and why?

3. **How does the student learn?** To meet the student's optimal learning needs:
   - What are the student's environmental preferences (i.e. noise, lighting, chairs, workspace, temperature)?
   - What is the student's preferred sensory input modality (i.e. visual, auditory, motor)?
   - How is the student smart (i.e. logic smart, music smart, body smart, picture smart, word smart, people smart, self smart, nature smart)?

4. **How does the student approach or react to an unfamiliar task?** When the student is learning something new, how are their behaviors affected by:
   - their cognitive style (i.e. impulsive/reflective, global/particular, leveler/sharpener, synthetic/analytic, inductive/deductive, concrete/abstract, random/sequential)?
   - their personality type (i.e. introvert/extrovert, sensory-intuitive, thinking-feeling, judging-perceiving)?
   - their motivation to learn (i.e. intrinsic, extrinsic)?
   - their choices and opportunities

5. **What will you do with the knowledge gained from answering the previous four questions?**
   - Will you consider linking students' interests with what they are reading?

Intervention Tracking Form for :_____ p.1

Content	Universal Screening	Specific Skill Areas of Concern	Classroom Intervention

Core Program
 	
Cardinal Questions—
**Learning Strengths
———Visual
———Auditory
———Motor-
     Kinesthetic
 	
Kind of Smart:
 	
_____
 	
**Behavioral Mindset
———Motivated
———Accepting
———Acts out
———Shuts down
———Diverts
     attention
 	
UDL Strategies
1.
 	
2.
 	
3.
	Date:
	
	Results
	
	Date:
	
	Results
	
	Date:
	
	Results
		1.
		
		2.
		
		3.
			Date:
			
			Target Area:
			
			Technique:
			
			Start date:
			
			Duration:
			
			Location
			
			Person(s) responsible
			
			Data to be collected
			
			Follow-up date
			
			Results:

Kemp & Eaton, 2007

Intervention Tier _____	Intervention Tier _____	Intervention Tier _____
Date:	Date:	Date:
Target Area:	Target Area:	Target Area:
Technique:	Technique:	Technique:
Start date:	Start date:	Start date:
Duration:	Duration:	Duration:
Location	Location	Location
Person(s) responsible	Person(s) responsible	Person(s) responsible
Data to be collected	Data to be collected	Data to be collected
Follow-up date	Follow-up date	Follow-up date
Results:	Results:	Results:

Kemp & Eaton, 2007

Response To Intervention Planning Document

Intensive Interventions

Intensive Interventions	Provider	Monitoring how often?			
1.					
2.					
3.					
4.					
5					

Targeted Interventions

Targeted Interventions	Provider	Monitoring how often?		
1.				
2.				
3.				
4.				
5				

Core Reading Program by Grade

Core Reading Program by Grade	Time - 90min			
K				
1				
2				
3				
4				
5				

Universal Screening:

Benchmark dates: Fall   Winter   Spring

Tier III
60m/
day
5-10%

Tier II
30 min/
2x wk

10-15%

Tier I
Core Reading and
Classroom
Interventions

85-90% of students
benefit

Kemp & Eaton, 2007

Planning Form

Teacher Key for _____

Technique # _____ **Description:** _____

Directions:

Sample __:	Sample __:	Sample __:	Sample __:
1.	1.	1.	1.
2.	2.	2.	2.
3.	3.	3.	3.
4.	4.	4.	4.
5.	5.	5.	5.
6.	6.	6.	6.
7.	7.	7.	7.
8.	8.	8.	8.
9.	9.	9.	9.
10.	10.	10.	10.
Sample __:	Sample __:	Sample __:	Sample __:
1.	1.	1.	1.
2.	2.	2.	2.
3.	3.	3.	3.
4.	4.	4.	4.
5.	5.	5.	5.
6.	6.	6.	6.
7.	7.	7.	7.
8.	8.	8.	8.
9.	9.	9.	9.
10.	10.	10.	10.

Kemp & Eaton 2007

Individual Tracking Progress Form

Student:			
Activity:			
Date:	**Date:**	**Date:**	**Date:**
1.	1.	1.	1.
2.	2.	2.	2.
3.	3.	3.	3.
4.	4.	4.	4.
5.	5.	5.	5.
6.	6.	6.	6.
7.	7.	7.	7.
8.	8.	8.	8.
9.	9.	9.	9.
10.	10.	10.	10.
% ___ /10	% ___ /10	% ___ /10	% ___ /10
Date:	**Date:**	**Date:**	**Date:**
1.	1.	1.	1.
2.	2.	2.	2.
3.	3.	3.	3.
4.	4.	4.	4.
5.	5.	5.	5.
6.	6.	6.	6.
7.	7.	7.	7.
8.	8.	8.	8.
9.	9.	9.	9.
10.	10.	10.	10.
% ___ /10	% ___ /10	% ___ /10	% ___ /10

Kemp & Eaton 2007

Group Tracking Progress:								
+								
-								
Comment								

Kemp & Eaton 2007

44 Phonemes of Standard American English

Phoneme	Some Sample Spelling(s) and Example Words	Phoneme	Some Sample Spelling(s) and Example Words
/ā/	a (table), a_e (bake), ai (train), ay (say)	/s/	s (say), c[e, i, y] (cent)
		/t/	t (time), t (bet), ed (flipped)
/ă/	a (flat), a_e (have)	/yū/	u (future), u_e (use), ew (few)
/b/	b (ball), b (knob)		
/k/	c (cake), k (key), ck (back)	/ŭ/	u (thumb), a (about), o (wagon)
/d/	d (door), d (bed)		
/ē/	e (me), ee (feet), ea (leap), y (baby)	/v/	v (voice), ve (give)
		/w/	w (wash)
/ĕ/	e (pet), ea (head)	/y/	y (yes)
/f/	f (fix), ph (phone), f (tough)	/z/	z (zoo), s (nose)
/g/	g (gas), g (bug)	/o͞o/	oo (boot), u (truth), u_e (rude), ew (chew)
/h/	h (hot)		
/ī/	I (I), i_e (bite), igh (light), y (sky)	/o͝o/	oo (book), u (put)
		/oi/	oi (soil), oy (toy)
/ĭ/	i (sit), y (gym)	/ou/	ou (out), ow (cow)
/j/	j (jet), dge (edge), g[e, i, y] (gem)	/aw/	aw (saw), au (caught), a[l] (tall)
/l/	l (lamp) , ll (fell)	/sh/	sh (ship), ti (nation), ci (special)
/m/	m (my), m (jam)		
/n/	n (no), kn (knock), n (pen)	/ch/	ch (chest), tch (catch)
/ō/	o (okay), o_e (bone), oa (soap), ow (low)	/th/	th (thick), th (with)
		/TH/	th (the), the (bathe)
/ŏ/	o (hot), a (watch)	/ng/	ng (sing), n (think)
/p/	p (pie), p (hop)	/zh/	s (measure), z (azure)
/r/	r (road), wr (wrong), er (her), ir (sir), ur (fur)	/D/	t (writer), dd (ladder), tt (letter), d (ladle)
/ar/	ar (car)		
/or/	oor (door), our (four)		
/ĕa/	ear (bear), are (share)		
/ēe/	eer (deer), ere (here), ear (fear)		

Closed

**vc
short V
ending C**

Open

**V — CV — CCV
usually ends with a long vowel
spelled with one letter**

C - le

unaccented final syllable a consonant plus [l] with a silent *e*

Vowel team/dipthong/digraph

2 vowels together + oi/oy + ou/ow

R - *controlled*

any syllable in which the vowel is followed by [r]

VCe

single vowel, a consonant, then silent *e*

Fluency—Paired Read Aloud Feedback Form

Partner Name: _____

After the 3rd reading, my partner: Compliments

- Read more words ☐

- Read smoother ☐

- Read with expression ☐

Kemp & Eaton 2007

Partner Name: _____

After the 3rd reading, my partner: Compliments

- Read more words ☐

- Read smoother ☐

- Read with expression ☐

Kemp & Eaton 2007

Fluency—Oral Reading Fluency Scale
Rubric for Assessment of Prosody

Level 4   Reads primarily in larger, meaningful phrase groups. Although some regressions, repetitions, and deviations from text may be present, these do not appear to detract from the overall structure of the story. Preservation of the author's syntax is consistent. Some or most of the story is read with expressive interpretation.

Level 3   Reads primarily in three- or four-word phrase groups. Some smaller groupings may be present. However, the majority of phrasing seems appropriate and preserves the syntax of the author. Little or no expressive interpretation is present.

Level 2   Reads primarily in two-word phrases with some three- or four-word groupings. Some word-by-word reading may be present. Word groupings may seem awkward and unrelated to larger context of sentence or passage.

Level 1   Reads primarily word-by-word. Occasional two-word or three-word phrases may occur-but these are infrequent and/or they do not preserve meaningful syntax.

A score of 1 should also be given to a student who reads with excessive speed, ignoring punctuation and other phrase boundaries, and reads with little or no expression.

Source: U.S. Department of Education, National Center for Education Statistics. *Listening to Children Read Aloud, 15.* Washington, DC: 1995.

Fluency—Data Collection Sheet

Name:					
Date:					
Passage					
Score wpm					
Date:					
Passage					
Score wpm					

Name:					
Date:					
Passage					
Score wpm					
Date:					
Passage					
Score wpm					

Kemp & Eaton 2007

Vocabulary—Frame 1, Visual Association

New word		Personal connection	
1		3	
Student-friendly definition		**Visual association**	
2		4	

New word		Personal connection	
1		3	
Student-friendly definition		**Visual association**	
2		4	

Kemp & Eaton, 2007

Vocabulary—Frame 2, Sentence Variation

New word	Personal connection (Draw or Write)
1	3
Student-friendly definition	Write a sentence about yourself using the word.
2	4

New word	Personal connection (Draw or Write)
1	3
Student-friendly definition	Write a sentence about yourself using the word.
2	4

Kemp & Eaton, 2007

Vocabulary—Frame 3, Example and Non-Example Variation

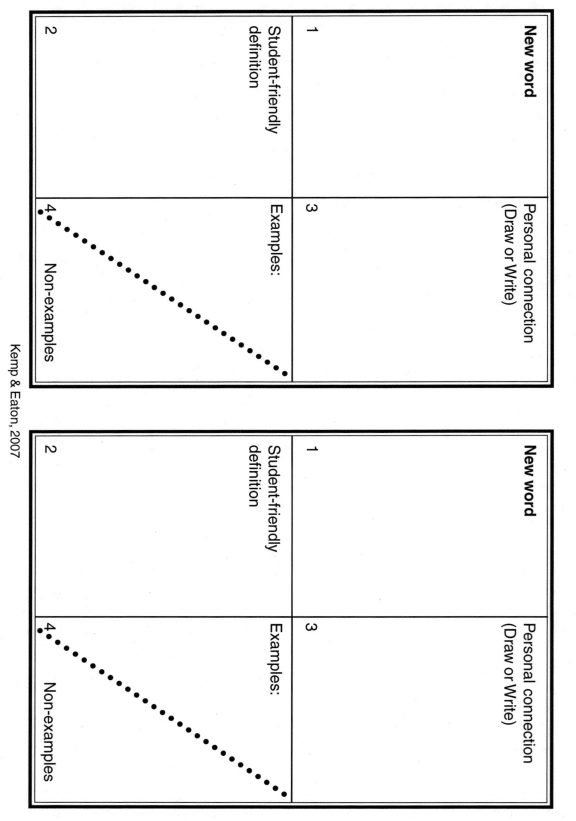

New word		Personal connection (Draw or Write)
Student-friendly definition	1	
	3	Examples:
2	4	Non-examples

New word		Personal connection (Draw or Write)
Student-friendly definition	1	
	3	Examples:
2	4	Non-examples

Kemp & Eaton, 2007

Vocabulary—Rehearsal Sheet Template

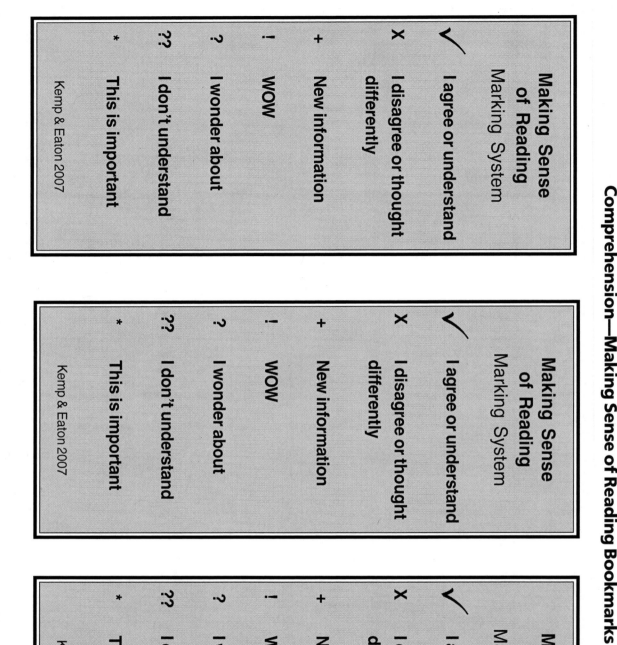

Making Sense of Reading
Marking System

✓   I agree or understand

✗   I disagree or thought differently

+   New information

!   WOW

?   I wonder about

??   I don't understand

*   This is important

Kemp & Eaton 2007

Making Sense of Reading
Marking System

✓   I agree or understand

✗   I disagree or thought differently

+   New information

!   WOW

?   I wonder about

??   I don't understand

*   This is important

Kemp & Eaton 2007

Making Sense of Reading
Marking System

✓   I agree or understand

✗   I disagree or thought differently

+   New information

!   WOW

?   I wonder about

??   I don't understand

*   This is important

Kemp & Eaton 2007

Comprehension—"Passage Essence" Steps

1. Read aloud one passage of selected text.

2. Read the selected text a second time and use a transparency pen to underline/highlight every **who** or **what** in the passage.

3. Use the "Passage Essence T-chart" transparency and list every **who** or **what** in the appropriate column.

4. Review the **who** or **what** column entries and determine the primary **who** or **what** of this reading selection.

5. Read the selected text a third time and underline/highlight the **most important thing(s) about** the **who or** the **what** in a different color.

6. List the **most important thing(s) about** the who or what in the appropriate column.

7. Synthesize (find similarities) the **most important things** about the who or what and combine ideas, actions, etc..

8. Using the **who** or **what** and **the most important things** about the who or what generate a main idea statement about the passage in ten words or less.

Steps to "Passage Essence"

1. Read aloud one passage of selected text.

2. Read the selected text a second time and use a transparency pen to **highlight** every **who** or **what** in the passage.

3. Use the "Passage Essence T-chart" transparency and **list** every **who** or **what** in the appropriate column.

4. **Review** the **who** or **what** column entries and **determine** the **primary** who or what of this reading selection.

5. Read the selected text a third time and **highlight** the **most important thing(s)** about the who or the what in a different color.

6. **List** the **most important thing(s)** about the who or what in the appropriate column.

7. **Synthesize** (find similarities) the **most important things** about the who or what and combine ideas, actions, etc..

8. Using the who or what and the most important things about the who or what **generate a main idea** statement about the passage **in ten words or less.**

Kemp & Eaton, 2007

Steps to "Passage Essence"

1. Read aloud one passage of selected text.

2. Read the selected text a second time and use a transparency pen to **highlight** every **who** or **what** in the passage.

3. Use the "Passage Essence T-chart" transparency and **list** every **who** or **what** in the appropriate column.

4. **Review** the **who** or **what** column entries and **determine** the **primary** who or what of this reading selection.

5. Read the selected text a third time and **highlight** the **most important thing(s)** about the who or the what in a different color.

6. **List** the **most important thing(s)** about the who or what in the appropriate column.

7. **Synthesize** (find similarities) the **most important things** about the who or what and combine ideas, actions, etc..

8. Using the who or what and the most important things about the who or what **generate a main idea** statement about the passage **in ten words or less.**

Kemp & Eaton, 2007

Comprehension—"Passage Essence" T-chart

Name:

Reading Selection:

Who or What...	The most important things about the Who or What...	
	From the Text	Synthesis
Primary who or what:		
Main Idea in ten words or less...		

Comprehension—Think Ahead Template

Think Ahead	Title/Topic:
Why am I reading this?	What comes to mind?
	What do I know about it?
What do I think the reading is about? Predictions 1. 2. 3. 4.	What in the reading supports this?

What do I want to think about as I am reading? Question 1
Question 2
Question 3
Question 4
Question 5
Kemp & Eaton, 2007

Comprehension—Think Ahead Checklist

Think Ahead Checklist	
1. Did I look at the title and write my thoughts?	
2. Did I think about my purpose for reading?	
3. Did I write at least 2 or 3 predictions?	
4. Did I write 3-4 questions I want answered from the reading?	
5. Am I ready to read the text?	
Kemp & Eaton, 2007	

Think Ahead Checklist	
1. Did I look at the title and write my thoughts?	
2. Did I think about my purpose for reading?	
3. Did I write at least 2 or 3 predictions?	
4. Did I write 3-4 questions I want answered from the reading?	
5. Am I ready to read the text?	
Kemp & Eaton, 2007	

Comprehension—Think Ahead/Wrap It Up Template

Think Ahead	*Wrap It Up*
Title/Topic: *Author:*	
What do I know about it? What comes to mind?	Was I right?
Why am I reading this?	How would I rate this book?
What do I think the reading is about? Predictions 1. 2. 3. 4.	What in the reading supports this?
What do I want to think about as I am reading? Question 1	Answered ?
Question 2	Answered ?
Question 3	Answered ?
Summary:	
Kemp & Eaton, 2007	

Comprehension—Topic Chart Template

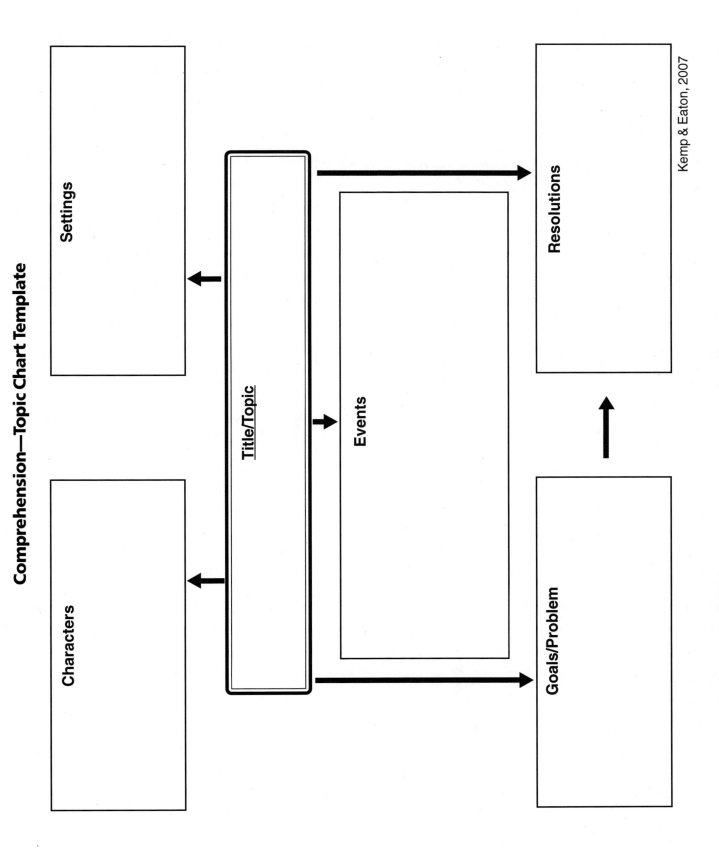

Settings

Characters

Title/Topic

Events

Resolutions

Goals/Problem

Kemp & Eaton, 2007

Comprehension—Topic Chart Template with Questions

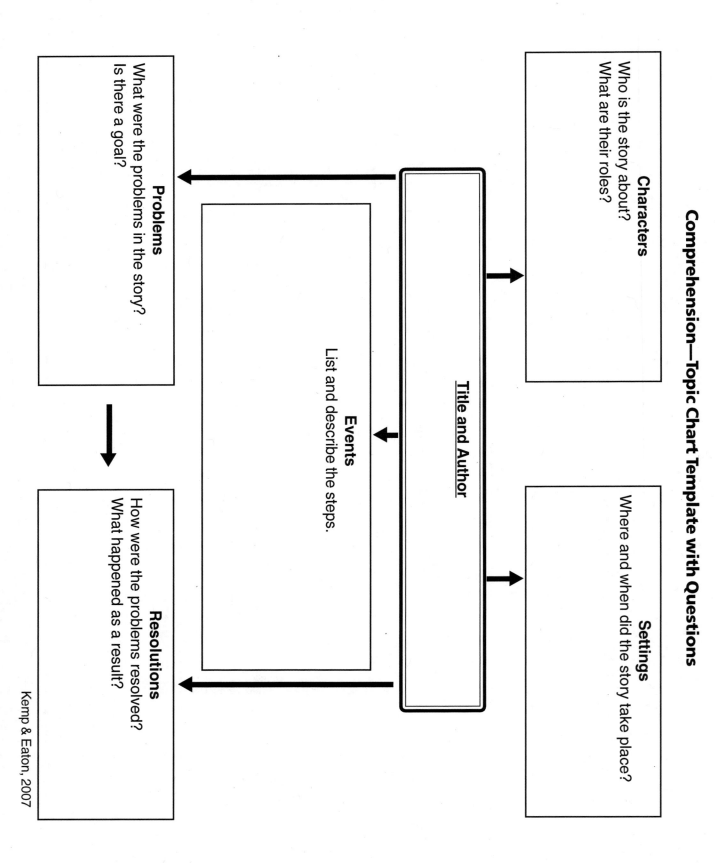

Characters
Who is the story about?
What are their roles?

Settings
Where and when did the story take place?

Title and Author

Events
List and describe the steps.

Problems
What were the problems in the story?
Is there a goal?

Resolutions
How were the problems resolved?
What happened as a result?

Kemp & Eaton, 2007

Motivation—Interest Survey

Please complete the survey about interests. Fill in the blanks that describe the things you like to do. After filling in the blanks, cut the survey apart so that you have a strip for each activity or interest. Discard the activities you do not like to do. Rank order your strips from most favorite (#1) to least favorite. Once you are happy with your interest ranking, number the strips. Remember #1 is your most favorite, # 2 is your next favorite and then transfer that information to a piece of paper. Write your name at the top of the paper. Thank you.

— —

Listening to music. My favorite is _____

— —

Hanging out with friends. Where? _____

— —

Playing video games. I'm really good at _____

— —

Playing/Watching sports. My favorite sport is _____

— —

Drawing and painting. I like to draw and paint _____

— —

Reading. I like to read _____

— —

Going to school. My favorite time at school is _____

— —

Surfing the net. I like _____

— —

Playing an instrument. I play _____

— —

Working on a hobby. My hobby is _____

— —

Watching movies. I just watched _____

— —

Watching television. My favorite TV show is _____

___ ___

Being outdoors in nature. I enjoy _____

___ ___

I really like _____

Kemp & Eaton, 2007

Motivation—Give Me a Grade Today Template

Give Me a Grade Today!

Today's lesson on _____
was _____

For your teaching today I would give you this grade: _____
because _____

I would benefit more from this lesson if: _____

_____

I still need _____

_____

Name: _____   Date: _____

Kemp & Eaton, 2007

Give Me a Grade Today!

Today's lesson on _____
was _____

For your teaching today I would give you this grade: _____
because _____

I would benefit more from this lesson if: _____

_____

I still need _____

_____

Name: _____   Date: _____

Kemp & Eaton, 2007

References

Adams, M. J. (1990). *Beginning to read*. Cambridge, MA.:MIT Press

Allington, R. L. (1993). Fluency: The neglected reading goal. *The Reading Teacher*, 556-561.

Armbruster, B. B., Lehr, F., Osborn, J. (2001). *Put reading first, The research building blocks for teaching children to read*. Partnership for Reading.

Baumann, J. F., & Kame'enui, E. J., (Eds.) (2004). *Vocabulary instruction*. (pp. 13-27). New York: Guilford Press.

Beck, I. L. (2006). *Making sense of phonics. The hows and whys*. New York: The Guilford Press.

Beck, I. L., McKeown, M.G., and Kucan, L. (2002). *Bringing words to life: Robust vocabulary instruction*. New York: The Guilford Press.

Becker, W. C. (1977). Teaching reading and language to the disadvantaged— What we have learned from field research. *Harvard Educational Review, 47*, 518-543.

Biemiller, A. (2003). Vocabulary: Needed if more children are to read well. *Reading Psychology, 24*(3-4), 323-335.

Blachman, B.A. (Ed.) (1997). *Foundations of reading acquisition and dyslexia: Implications for early intervention*. (pp. 243- 264). Mahwah, NJ: Lawrence Erlbaum Associates.

Blakey, E., & Spence, S. (1990). Developing metacognition. *ERIC Digest* [Online]. Available: http://www.eric.ed.gov/contentdelivery/servlet/ ERICServlet?accno=ED327218

Blevins, W. (1998). *Phonics from A to Z, a practical guide*. New York: Scholastic.

Block, C. C., & Pressley. M., (Eds.). (2002). *Comprehension instruction: Research-based best practices*. New York: The Guilford Press.

Burns, M. K., Tucker, J. A., Hauser, A., Thelen, R, L., Holmes, K J., White, K. (2002). Minimum reading fluency rate necessary for comprehension: A potential criterion for curriculum-based assessments. *Assessment for Effective Intervention, 28*(1), 1-7.

Catts, H. W. (1997). The early identification of language-based learning disabilities. *Language, Speech, and Hearing Services in Schools. 28*, 86-89.

Clymer, T. (1963). Utility of phonics generalization in the primary grades. *The Reading Teacher, 16.*

Csikszentmihalyi, M. (1990). *Flow: The psychology of optimal experience.* New York: Harper & Row.

Cummins, J. (1979). *Cognitive/academic language proficiency, linguistic interdependence, the optimum age question and some other matters.* Working Papers on Bilingualism, 19, 121-129.

Deno, S.L. (2003). Developments in curriculum-based measurement. *The Journal of Special Education,* 37(3), 184-192(9).

Fielding, L., & Pearson, D. P. (1994). Reading comprehension: What works? *Educational Leadership, 51*(5), 62-67.

Finn, C. E., Rotherham, A. J., and Hokanson, C. R. (Eds.) (2001) *Rethinking Special Education For a New Century.* Washington, D.C.: Progressive Policy Institute and Thomas B. Fordham Foundation.

Ford, M. (1992). *Motivating humans.* Newbury Park, CA: Sage Publications.

Francis, D., Shaywitz, S., Stuebing, K., Shaywitz, B., & Fletcher, J. (1996). Developmental lag versus deficit models of reading disability: A longitudinal, individual growth curves analysis. *Journal of Educational Psychology,* 88(1), 3-17.

Fuchs, L. S., Fuchs, D., Hamlett, C. L., Walz, L., & Germann, G. (1993). Formative evaluation of academic progress: How much growth can we expect? *School Psychology Review,* 22, 27-48.

Good, III, R.H., Simmons D.C., and Kame'enui E.J. (2001). The importance of decision-making utility of a continuum of fluency-based indicators of foundational reading skills for third-grade high-stakes outcomes. *Scientific Studies of Reading*; 5(3), 257–288.

Grossen, B. (1997). *The National Right to Read Foundation, A synthesis of research on reading from the National Institute of Child Health and Human Development*, University of Oregon.

Hart, B., & Risley, T.R. (1995). *Meaningful differences in the everyday experience of young American children.* Baltimore: Paul H. Brooks Publishing Co.

Hasbrouck, J. & Gerald A. Tindal, G. A. (2006) Oral Reading Fluency Norms: A Valuable Assessment Tool for Reading Teachers. *The Reading Teacher, 59*(7), 636.

Hiebert, E. H. & Kamil, M. L. Eds. (2005). *Teaching and Learning Vocabulary: Bringing Research to Practice.* Mahwah, NJ: Erlbaum.

Horner, R., & Sugai, G. (1999). Discipline and behavioral support: Practices, pitfalls and promises. *Effective School Practices, 17*(4), 65-71.

Hosp, M K., Hosp, J. L., & Howell, K.W. (2007). *The ABC's of CBM, A practical guide to curriculum-based measurement.* New York: The Guilford Press.

Jenkins, J.R., Fuchs, L.S., van den Broek, P., Espin, C., Deno, S.L. (2003). Sources of individual differences of reading comprehension and reading fluency. *Journal of Educational Psychology, 95,* 719-725.

Jensen, E. (1998). *Teaching with the brain in mind.* Association for Supervision and Curriculum Development.

Lehr, F., Osborn, J., & Hiebert, E. H., *A focus on vocabulary.* Pacific Resources for Education and Learning (internet download 2/10/07).

Lindsley, O.R. (2004). *Ogden R. Lindsley (1922-2004): Publications.* Retreived April 8, 2007, from http://www.fluency.org.

Lindsley, O. R. (1992). Precision teaching: Discoveries and effects. *Journal of Applied Behaviour Analysis, 25,* 51-57.

Lindsley, O. R. (1990) Precision Teaching: By teachers for children. *Teaching Exceptional Children, 22*(3), 10-15.

Lopate, P. (1975). *Being with children.* New York: Simon & Schuster.

Lovitt, T. C., & Hansen, C. L. (1976). The use of contingent skipping and drilling to improve oral reading and comprehension. *Journal of Learning Disabilities, 9,* 481-487.

Lyon, G. R. (2002). *Learning disabilities and early intervention strategies: How to reform the special education referral and identification process.* Hearing before the Subcommittee on Education Reform Committee on Education and the Workforce United States House of Representatives.

Lyon, G. R. (2004).*The NICHD research program in reading development, reading disorders, and reading instruction initiated: 1965.* Paper presented at the 31st annual conference of the New York Branch of the International Dyslexia Association.

Moats, L.C. (1999). Teaching reading is rocket science: What expert teachers of reading should know and be able to do. *American Educator,* June.

Moats, L.C. (2000). *Speech to print: Language essentials for teachers.* Baltimore: Paul H. Brooks Publishing Co.

National Center for Education Statistics. (2003). *National assessment of educational progress: The nation's report card.* Washington, DC: U.S. Department of Education.

National Institute of Child, Health, and Human Development (NICHD). (2000). Report of the National Reading Panel. *Teaching children to read: An evidence-based assessment of the scientific research literature on reading and its implications for reading instruction.* Available online at: http://www.nichd.nih.gov/publications/nrp/smallbook.htm.

Pinnell, G. S., Pikulski, J. J., Wixson, K. K., Campbell, J. R., Gough, P. B., & Beatty, A. S. (1995). *Listening to children read aloud: Oral fluency.* Washington, DC: U.S. Department of Education, National Center for Education Statistics.

Pressley, M. (2001). Comprehension instruction: What makes sense now, what might make sense soon. *Reading Online, 5*(2). Available: http://www.readingonline.org/articles.

Rasinski, T. V., (2002). Speed does matter in reading. *Scholastic Red*. Retrieved on May 31, 2007 from www.scholasticred.com.

Rasinski, T.V. (2003). *The fluent reader*. New York: Scholastic Professional Books.

Shaywitz, S., Shaywitz, B., et al. (1990). "Prevalence of reading disability in boys and girls: Results of the Connecticut Longitudinal Study." *Journal of the American Medical Association*, 264(8), 998-1002.

Shinn, M. R., Baker, S., Habedank, L., Good, R. H. (1993). The effects of classroom reading performance data on general education teachers' and parents' attitudes about reintegration. *Exceptionality*, Vol. 4, No. 4, Pages 205-228.

Simon, C. (Ed.) (1995). Communication skills and classroom success: Therapy methodologies for language learning disabled students (pp 199-260). Boston: Little, Brown.

Stahl, S. A., & Fairbanks, M. M. (1986). The effects of vocabulary instruction: A model-based meta-analysis. *Review of Educational Research 56*(1), 72-110.

Stahl, S. A. (2003). Words are learned incrementally over multiple exposures. *American Educator, 27*(1), 18-19, 44. Free online at http://www.aft.org/pubsreports/american_educator/spring2003/stahl.html.

Starlin, C. M. (1982). On Reading and Writing. Iowa Monograph.

Stecker, P.M., Fuchs, L.S. & Fuchs, D. (2005). Using curriculum-based measurement to improve student achievement: *Review of Research Psychology in the Schools.* 42(8), 795-819.

Thomas, A., & Grimes, J. (Eds.) (2002). *Best practices in school psychology* (Vol. 4, pp. 671-697). Silver Spring, MD: National Association of School Psychologists.

Torgesen, J. K. (2004). Preventing early reading failure: Evidence for early intervention. *American Educator*, Fall, 2004.

Van Kleek, A. (1990). Emergent literacy: Learning about print before learning to read. *Topics in Language Disorders*, 10(2), 25-45.

Vaughn, J. L. & Estes, T. H. (1986). Reading and reasoning beyond the primary grades. Boston: Allyn & Bacon.

Walsch, N. D. (1996). Conversations with god: An uncommon dialogue. New York: G.P. Putnam's Sons.

Willingham, D. (2007). Reading Comprehension, EdNews.org (internet download, 2/25/07).

Wright, J. (2007). The RTI tool kit: A practical guide for schools. New York: National Professional Resources, Inc..

Resources: Print and Video Materials
Available from National Professional Resources, Inc.
1-800 453-7461 • www.NPRinc.com

Allington, Richard L. & Patricia M. Cunningham. (1996). *Schools That Work: Where all Children Read and Write.* New York, NY: Harper Collins.

Armstrong, Thomas. *(1996). Beyond the ADD Myth: Classroom Strategies & Techniques* (Video). Port Chester, NY: National Professional Resources, Inc.

Armstrong, Thomas. (1997). *The Myth of the A.D.D. Child.* New York, NY: Penguin Putnam Inc.

ASCD. (2006). *Teaching Students with Learning Disabilities in the Regular Classroom* (Video). Baltimore, MD: ASDC.

Barnett, D.W., Daly, E.J., Jones, K.M., & Lentz, F.E. (2004). *Response to intervention: Empirically based special service decisions from single-case designs of increasing and decreasing intensity. Journal of Special Education*, 38, 66-79.

Basso, Dianne, & Natalie McCoy. (2002). *The Co-Teaching Manual.* Columia, SC: Twin Publications.

Bateman, Barbara D. & Annemieke Golly. (2003). *Why Johnny Doesn't Behave: Twenty Tips for Measurable BIPs*. Verona, WI: Attainment Company, Inc.

Bateman, Barbara D. & Cynthia M. Herr. (2003). *Writing Measurable IEP Goals and Objectives*. Verona, WI: Attainment Company, Inc.

Beecher, Margaret. (1995). *Developing the Gifts & Talents of All Students in the Regular Classroom.* Mansfield Center, CT: Creative Learning Press, Inc.

Bender, William. *Differentiating Instruction for Students with Learning Disabilities*. Thousand Oaks, CA: Corwin Press, 2002.

Bray, Marty & Abbie Brown, et al. (2004). *Technology and the Diverse Learner.* Thousand Oaks, CA: Corwin Press.

Brown-Chidsey, Rachel & Mark W. Steege. (2005). *Response to Intervention*. New York, NY: Guilford Press.

Casbarro, Joseph. (2005). *Test Anxiety & What You Can Do About It: A Practical Guide for Teachers, Parents, & Kids.* Port Chester, NY: Dude Publishing.

Chapman, Carolyn & Rita King. (2003). *Differentiated Instructional Strategies for Reading in the Content Areas.* Thousand Oaks, CA: Corwin Press.

Council for Exceptional Children and Merrill Education. (2005). *Universal Design for Learning*. Atlanta, GA.

Crone, Deanne A. & Robert H. Horner. (2003). *Building Positive Behavior Support Systems in Schools: Functional Behavioral Assessment.* New York, NY: Guilford Press.

Deiner, Penny Low. (2004). *Resources for Educating Children with Diverse Abilities, 4th Edition.* Florence, KY: Thomson Delmar Learning.

Deshler, Donald D. & Jean B. Schumaker. (2005). *Teaching Adolescents With Disabilities: Accessing the General Education Curriculum.* Thousand Oaks, CA: Corwin Press.

Dieker, Lisa. (2006). *7 Effective Strategies for Secondary Inclusion (Video).* Port Chester, NY: National Professional Resources, Inc.

Dieker, Lisa. (2006). *Co-Teaching Lesson Plan Book (Third Edition).* Whitefish Bay, WI: Knowledge By Design.

Dodge, Judith. (2005). *Differentiation in Action*. Jefferson City, MO: Scholastic Inc., 2005.

Elias, Maurice & Linda B. Butler. (2005). *Social Decision Making/Social Problem Solving A Curriculum for Academic, Social and Emotional Learning.* Champaign, IL: Research Press.

Elias, Maurice, Brian Friedlander & Steven Tobias. (2001). *Engaging the Resistant Child Through Computers: A Manual to Facilitate Social & Emotional Learning*. Port Chester, NY: Dude Publishing.

Elias, Maurice & Harriett Arnold. (2006). *The Educator's Guide to Emotional Intelligence and Academic Achievement.* Thousand Oaks, CA: Corwin Press.

Elliott, Judy L. & Martha L. Thurlow. (2000). *Improving Test Performance of Students with Disabilities. On District and State Assessments.* Thousand Oaks, CA: Corwin Press.

Fad, Kathleen McConnell & James R. Patton. (2000). *Behavioral Intervention Planning.* Austin, TX: Pro-Ed, Inc.

Friedlander, Brian S. (2005). *Assistive Technology: A Way to Differentiate Instruction for Students with Disabilities.* Port Chester, NY: National Professional Resources, Inc.

Friend, Marilyn. (2004). *The Power of Two: Making a Difference Through Co-Teaching, 2nd Edition* (Video). Bloomington, IN: Forum on Education.

Fuchs, D., Mock, D., Morgan, P., & Young, C. (2003). *Responsiveness-to-intervention: Definitions, evidence, and implications for learning disabilities construct. Learning Disabilities: Research and Practice*, 18(3), 157-171.

Fuchs, L. (2003). *Assessing intervention responsiveness: conceptual and technical issues.* Learning Disabilities Research & Practice, 18(3), 172-186.

Fuchs, L.S., & Fuchs, D. (2006). A framework for building capacity for responsiveness to intervention. *School Psychology Review*, 35, 621-626.

Gardner, Howard. (1996). *How Are Kids Smart?* (Video) Port Chester, NY: National Professional Resources, Inc.

Glasser, William. (1998). *Choice Theory: A New Psychology of Personal Freedom.* New York, NY: HarperCollins.

Gold, Mimi. (2003). *Help for the Struggling Student: Ready-to-Use Strategies and Lessons to Build Attention, Memory, and Organizational Skills.* San Francisco, CA: Jossey-Bass.

Goleman, Daniel. (1996). *Emotional Intelligence: A New Vision for Educators* (Video). Port Chester, NY: National Professional Resources, Inc.

Good, R.H. & Kaminski, R.A. (2001). *Dynamic indicators of basic early literacy skills* (6th ed.). Eugene, OR: Institute for the Development of Educational Achievement.

Gorman, Jean Cheng. (2001). *Emotional Disorders and Learning Disabilities in the Classroom: Interactions and Interventions.* Thousand Oaks, CA: Corwin Press.

Gregory, Gale & Carolyn Chapman. (2002). *Differentiated Instructional Strategies: One Size Doesn't Fit All.* Thousand Oaks, CA: Corwin Press.

Gresham, F.M. (2001). *Responsiveness to intervention: An alternative approach to the identification of learning disabilities.* Paper presented at the Learning Disabilities Summit, Washington, DC.

Grimes, J., & Kurns, S. (2003, December). *An intervention-based system for addressing NCLB and IDEA expectations: A multiple tiered model to ensure every child learns.* Paper presented at the National Research Center on Learning Disabilities Responsiveness-to-Intervention Symposium, Kansas City, MO.

Guilford Press (Producer). (1999). *Assessing ADHD in the Schools* (Video). New York, NY.

Guilford Press (Producer). (1999). *Classroom Interventions for ADHD* (Video). New York, NY.

Gusman, Jo. (2004). *Differentiated Instruction & the English Language Learner: Best Practices to Use With Your Students (K-12)* (Video). Port Chester, NY: National Professional Resources, Inc.

Heacox, Diane. (2002). *Differentiated Instruction: How to Reach and Teach All Learners (Grades 3-12).* Minneapolis, MN: Free Spirit Press.

Hehir, Thomas. (2005). *New Directions in Special Education.* Cambridge, MA: Harvard University Press.

Iervolino, Constance & Helene Hanson. (2003). *Differentiated Instructional Practice Video Series: A Focus on Inclusion (Tape 1), A Focus on the Gifted (Tape 2).* Port Chester, NY: National Professional Resources, Inc.

Jensen, Eric. (2000). *Different Brains, Different Learners: How to Reach the Hard to Reach.* San Diego, CA: The Brain Store.

Jensen, Eric. (2000).*The Fragile Brain: What Impairs Learning and What We Can Do About It.* Port Chester, NY: National Professional Resources, Inc.

Jensen, Eric. (2000). *Practical Applications of Brain-Based Learning.* Port Chester, NY: National Professional Resources, Inc.

Kagan, Spencer & Laurie Kagan. (1999). *Reaching Standards Through Cooperative Learning: Providing for ALL Learners in General Education Classrooms* (4-video series). Port Chester, NY: National Professional Resources, Inc.

Kagan, Spencer & Miguel Kagan. (1998). *Multiple Intelligences: The Complete MI Book.* San Clemente, CA: Kagan Cooperative Learning.

Kame'enui, Edward J. & Deborah C. Simmons. (1999). *Adapting Curricular Materials, Volume 1: An Overview of Materials Adaptations—Toward Successful Inclusion of Students with Disabilities: The Architecture of Instruction.* Reston, VA: Council for Exceptional Children.

Katzman, Lauren I. & Allison G. Gandhi (Editors). (2005). *Special Education for a New Century.* Cambridge, MA: Harvard Educational Review.

Kemp, Karen. (2007). *RTI Tackles Reading* (Video). Port Chester, NY: National Professional Resources, Inc.

Kemp, Karen. (2007). *RTI: The Classroom Connection.* Port Chester, NY: Dude Publishing.

Kennedy, Eugene. (2003). *Raising Test Scores for All Students: An Administrator's Guide to Improving Standardized Test Performance.* Thousand Oaks, CA: Corwin Press.

Kleinert, Harold L. & Jacqui F. Kearns. (2001). *Alternate assessment: Measuring Outcomes and Supports for Students with Disabilities.* Baltimore, MD: Brookes Publishing Company, Inc.

Lavoie, Richard. (2005). *Beyond F.A.T. City* (Video). Charlotte, NC: PBS Video.

Lavoie, Richard. (1989). *F.A.T. City: How Difficult Can This Be?* (Video). Charlotte, NC: PBS Video.

Lavoie, Richard.(2005). *It's So Much Work to Be Your Friend* (Video). Charlotte, NC: PBS Video.

Levine, Mel. (2002). *A Mind at a Time.* New York, NY: Simon & Schuster.

Lickona, Thomas. (2004). *Character Matters.* New York, NY: Touchstone.

Long, Nicholas, & William Morse. (1996). *Conflict in the Classroom: The Education of At-Risk and Troubled Students, 5th Edition.* Austin, TX: Pro-Ed, Inc.

Maanum, Jody L. (2003). *The General Educator's Guide to Special Education, 2nd Edition.* Minnetonka, MN: Peytral Publications, Inc.

Marston, D., Muyskens, P., Lau, M., & Canter, A. (2003). *Problem-Solving model for decision making with high-incidence: The Minneapolis experience.* Learning Disabilities Research and Practice, 18(3), 187-200.

McCarney, Stephen B. (1993). *The Pre-Referral Intervention Manual.* Columbia, MO: Hawthorne Educational Services.

McDougal, J.L., Clonan, S.M. & Martens, B.K. (2000). Using organizational change procedures to promote the acceptability of prereferral intervention services: The School-based Intervention Team Project. *School Psychology Quarterly*, 15, 149-171.

Minskoff, Esther & David Allsopp. (2002). *Academic Success Strategies for Adolescents with Learning Disabilities & ADHD.* Baltimore, MD: Paul H. Brookes Publishing.

Moll, Anne M. (2003). *Differentiated Instruction Guide for Inclusive Teaching.* Port Chester, NY: Dude Publishing.

Munk, Dennis D. (2003). *Solving the Grading Puzzle for Students with Disabilities.* Whitefish Bay, WI: Knowledge by Design, Inc.

National Association of State Directors of Special Education (NASDSE). (2005). *Response to Intervention: Policy, Considerations, and Implementation.* Alexandria, VA: NASDSE.

Nelsen, Jane, Lynn Lott & H. Stephen Glenn. (2000). *Positive Discipline In The Classroom: Developing Mutual Respect, Cooperation, and Responsibility in Your Classroom.* Three Rivers, MI: Three Rivers Press.

Nolet, Victor & Margaret McLaughlin. (2000). *Accessing the General Curriculum: Including Students with Disabilities in Standards-Based Reform.* Thousand Oaks, CA: Corwin Press.

Norlander, Karen. (2006). *RTI Tackles the LD Explosion: A Good IDEA Becomes Law (Video).* Port Chester, NY: National Professional Resources, Inc.

Purcell, Sherry & Debbie Grant. (2004). *Using Assistive Technology to Meet Literacy Standards.* Verona, WI: IEP Resources.

Reider, Barbara. (2005). *Teach More and Discipline Less.* Thousand Oaks, CA: Corwin Press.

Renzulli, Joseph S. (1999). *Developing the Gifts and Talents of ALL Students: The Schoolwide Enrichment Model* (Video). Port Chester, NY: National Professional Resources, Inc.

Rief, Sandra F. (1998). *The ADD/ADHD Checklist.* Paramus, NJ: Prentice Hall.

Rief, Sandra F. (2004). *ADHD & LD: Powerful Teaching Strategies & Accommodations* (Video). Port Chester, NY: National Professional Resources, Inc.

Rief, Sandra F. (1997). *How to Help Your Child Succeed in School: Strategies and Guidance for Parents of Children with ADHD and/or Learning Disabilities* (Video). Port Chester, NY: National Professional Resources, Inc.

Rief, Sandra F. & Julie A. Heimburge. (1996). *How to Reach & Teach All Students in the Inclusive Classroom: Ready-To-Use Strategies, Lessons, and Activities for Teaching Students with Learning Needs.* West Nyack, NY: Center for Applied Research in Education.

Robinson, Viviane & Mei K. Lai. (2006). *Practitioner Research for Educators.* Thousand Oaks, CA: Corwin Press.

Rose, D. & A. Meyer (Editors). (2002). *Teaching Every Student in the Digital Age.* Alexandria, VA: ASCD.

Rose, D. & A. Meyer (Editors). (2005). *The Universally Designed Classroom: Accessible Curriculum and Digital Technologies.* Cambridge, MA: Harvard University Press.

Rutherford, Paula. (2002). *Instruction for All Students.* Alexandria, VA: Just Ask Publications.

Sailor, Wayne. (2004). *Creating A Unified System: Integrating General and Special Education for the Benefit of All Students* (Video). Bloomington, IN: Forum on Education.

Sailor, Wayne. (2002). *Whole-School Success and Inclusive Education: Building Partnerships for Learning, Achievement, and Accountability.* New York, NY: Teachers College Press.

Salovey, Peter. (1998). *Optimizing Intelligences: Thinking, Emotion, and Creativity* (Video). Port Chester, NY: National Professional Resources, Inc.

Shaywitz, Sally. (2003). *Overcoming Dyslexia: A New and Complete Science-Based Program for Reading Problems at Any Level.* New York, NY: Knopf Publishing.

Shinn, M. (1989). *Curriculum-based measurement: Assessing special children.* New York: Guilford Press.

Shumm, Jeanne Shay. (1999). *Adapting Curricular Materials, Volume 2: Kindergarten Through Grade Five—Adapting Reading & Math Materials for the Inclusive Classroom*. Reston, VA: Council for Exceptional Children.

Smith, Sally. (2001). *Teach Me Different!* (Video). Charlotte, NC: PBS Video.

Snell, Martha E. & Rachel Janney. (2000). *Collaborative Teaming*. Baltimore, MD: Paul H. Brookes Publishing Co., Inc.

Snell, Martha E. & Rachel Janney. (2000). *Social Relationships & Peer Support*. Baltimore, MD: Paul H. Brookes Publishing Co., Inc.

Sousa, David A. (2001). *How the Special Needs Brain Learns.* Thousand Oaks, CA: Corwin Press.

Sprick, R.S., Borgmeier, C., & Nolet, V. (2002). *Prevention and management of behavior problems in secondary schools*. In M.A. Shinn, H.M. Walker & G. Stoner (Eds.), *Interventions for academic and behavior problems II: Preventative and remedial approaches* (pp. 373-401). Bethesda, MD: National Association for School Psychologists.

Strichart, Stephen S., Charles T. Mangrum II & Patricia Iannuzzi. (1998). *Teaching Study Skills* and Strategies to Students with Learning Disabilities, Attention Deficit Disorders, *or Special Needs, 2nd Edition.* Boston, MA: Allyn & Bacon, 1998.

Thompson, Sandra, Rachel Quenemeen, Martha Thurlow, & James Ysseldyke. (2001). *Alternate Assessments for Students with Disabilities.* Thousand Oaks, CA: Corwin Press.

Thurlow, Martha L., Judy L. Elliott & James E. Ysseldyke. (1998). *Testing Students with Disabilities: Practical Strategies for Complying With District and State Requirements.* Thousand Oaks, CA: Corwin Press.

Tilton, Linda. (2003). *Teacher's Toolbox for Differentiating Instruction: 700 Strategies, Tips, Tools, & Techniques.* Shorewood, MN: Covington Cove Publications.

Tomlinson, Carol Ann. (2001). *How to Differentiate Instruction in Mixed-Ability Classrooms, 2nd Edition.* Alexandria, VA: ASCD.

Villa, Richard A. & Jacqueline S. Thousand. (2004). *A Guide to Co-Teaching.* Thousand Oaks, CA: Corwin Press.

Watson, T. Steuart & Mark W. Steege. (2003). *Conducting School-Based Functional Behavioral Assessments: A Practitioner's Guide.* New York, NY: Guilford Press.

Witt, J., & Beck, R. (1999). *One minute academic functional assessment and interventions: "Can't do it… or "won't" do it?* Longmont, CO: Sopris West.

Wood, M. Mary & Nicholas Long. (1991). *Life Space Intervention: Talking with Children and Youth in Crisis.* Austin, TX: Pro-Ed, Inc.

Wormel, Rick. *(2006). Fair Isn't Always Equal. Portland*, ME: Stenhouse Publishers.

Wright, J. (2007). *RTI Toolkit.* Port Chester, NY: National Professional Resources, Inc.

Wunderlich, Kathy C. (1988). *The Teacher's Guide to Behavioral Interventions.* Columbia, MO: Hawthorne Educational Services, Inc.

"These are the last words I have to say,
That's why this took so long to write.
There will be other words some other day,
But that's the story of my life."
—Billy Joel, *Famous Last Words*

About the Authors

Karen A. Kemp is a 30-year public school teaching veteran with a striking level of depth in her circulation and experience as a staff developer. She has presented workshops on a wide variety of topics in numerous locations around the United States and Europe, and has held a number of leadership and administrative positions, including Director of Special Education, Assistant Principal, Pupil Services Coordinator, Adjunct Faculty, Program Specialist, and, of course, classroom teacher. She has authored and co-authored over 30 publications on various educational topics including the books *Cool Kids: A Proactive Approach to Social Responsibility* and *TGIF: But What Will I Do On Monday?*, and the video series *Translating Research Into Practice (TRIP)*. Karen continues to provide professional development in the areas of RTI, Curriculum Based Measurement, Positive Behavior Supports and Active Participation Strategies. She is currently the Director of Special Programs in Cohoes City Schools in New York.

Mary Ann Eaton, M.S., CCC-S, is a certified Speech & Language Pathologist with over 30 years experience in the public schools of New York's Capital Region. Her vast school-based teaching experiences include pre-school through high school aged students. Mary Ann is a Professional Development Specialist skilled in utilizing the Problem Solving Process to evaluate School Report Cards and design professional staff development that addresses the needs of districts. She has presented at the state and national level. Mary Ann is currently an associate with The MAPLE Group and provides training and consultation to school districts in the areas of literacy, co-teaching, differentiated instruction, communication skills, and RTI.